Liars'
Room

Don't miss any of Dan Poblocki's spooky stories!

Liars'
Room

DAN POBLOCKI

SCHOLASTIC PRESS · NEW YORK

All rights reserved. Published by Scholastic
Press, an imprint of Scholastic Inc., *Publishers
since 1920*. SCHOLASTIC, SCHOLASTIC PRESS,
and associated logos are trademarks and/or
registered trademarks of Scholastic Inc.

The publisher does not have any control over and
does not assume any responsibility for author or
third-party websites or their content.

This book is a work of fiction. Names, characters,
places, and incidents are either the product of
the author's imagination or are used fictitiously,
and any resemblance to actual persons, living or
dead, business establishments, events, or locales
is entirely coincidental.

Library of Congress Cataloging-in-Publication
Data available

ISBN 978-0-545-83007-2

1 2021

Printed in the U.S.A. 23
First edition, November 2021

Book design by Christopher Stengel

This book is dedicated to my almost-twin sister, Emily, who's so very talented at helping me turn on all the lights.

"Lies are curses, and curses are lies."

— *Glynn Washington, host of* Spooked,

From episode S5E14

CHAPTER ONE
STELLA

STELLA HILL WAS rinsing a bowl in the sink when her stepbrother burst into the kitchen and shouted, "There's a ghost in the basement!" The bowl slipped from her grip, hit the basin, and cracked in half.

"Simon! Look what you made me do!" she shouted.

He wore a wild expression, eyes wide, mouth stretched into a grimace. His fingers were curled into fists, and his chest heaved as if he'd just run around all three wings of their new house in record time. If he was trying to scare her, which he probably was, he was doing an excellent job.

Stella's mom and her twin brother, Alex, rushed in from the dining room. "What's the ruckus?" Mom asked, glancing at the broken bowl in the sink.

Stella felt her face go red.

"There's a ghost in the basement!" Simon exclaimed again. "A real live ghost!"

"Ghosts aren't real or alive," Alex quipped.

Simon huffed, ready to argue, but Mom stepped in. "You know the basement is off-limits." Since coming to Frost Meadow, Stella's mother had become an expert in handling her stepson's moods. "Why did you go down there?"

"I heard a voice."

Alex stifled a laugh. Stella threw him a look.

Mom glanced at the twins. "Was it either of you?" They shook their heads. "Could it have been the radio, Simon? The television? Maybe there's someone outside — "

"It *wasn't* the radio." His voice edged toward a grumble. "It was a real voice. Coming from the basement. I went to check it out."

Mom sighed. "It's not safe down there. Your father and I — "

Simon held out both hands to her. "Won't you come see for yourself?"

For a moment, Stella thought he looked like an actual little kid and not the monster she'd known him to be.

"When we say it's not safe, buddy, we mean for *everyone*. There's exposed wire. Pieces of loose foundation. And junk from the old owner is all over the place. You could trip and split your head open."

"Mom, that's really gross," said Stella.

Mom pursed her lips. "Why don't you tell us what happened," she said to Simon.

The four sat around the kitchen table. As Simon went on with his latest tale of ghostly intrigue, Stella concentrated on her notepad, which lay open to a sketch she'd been working on during breakfast. She'd seen the image in a dream — a majestic white horse in a field of red roses. It was an idea for a mural on her bedroom wall. But looking at it now, she realized that the poor horse looked trapped. Starting over on her sketch, she barely listened as Simon went on. She knew he was trying to scare her. Alex always said it was best to just ignore him.

Simon had never been a friend to the twins, even before their parents had gotten married. Now in this new house where the two families had become one, he seemed determined to frighten the bejesus out of them all. Every week since the move, he'd come up with another "true" ghost story about the estate. Wildwyck was a spooky building to begin with, but Mom and Charlie had bought it hoping to convert each wing into charming, *un*-spooky town houses they'd eventually sell. Stella and Alex had had many conversations about Simon before their parents' wedding earlier that year, and now Stella worried that their worst fears about him were coming true.

She couldn't understand why he did the horrible things that he did. For attention? For revenge? Because he didn't know any better?

Her first bad experience with her stepbrother had been at a Christmas party in Brooklyn several years back. Charlie had come from Ohio to visit for the week, and he'd brought Simon with him for the first time. Simon's older brother, Zachary, had stayed in Columbus with their mother. The night of the party, the twins had been hiding out in Alex's room when Simon swept in through the doorway.

"What's happening?" he asked, putting on a silly, deep voice.

Alex was quick to wipe away tears. He and Stella had been discussing how much they missed their dad at that time of year. "We were chatting," Stella answered quietly, hoping he'd take the hint and go away.

At that point, she didn't know that Simon was the type of kid who needed more than a hint. "About what?"

"Why are you so interested in what we're doing?" Alex asked, annoyed.

"Because you didn't *invite* me." Simon smirked.

Stella didn't want to hurt his feelings. "Sometimes me and Alex just need to be alone together."

"That's weird," Simon went on. He picked up one of Alex's models from a shelf — a large Japanese mecha. The colorful humanoid robot was made of many detailed plastic pieces that Alex and his dad had spent nearly a week carefully gluing together.

"Don't touch that," Alex said, standing.

"I'm just looking at it."

"Put it down!"

Simon smiled. "Why are you getting so upset? It's just a toy."

"It's not just a toy," Alex insisted. "You have no idea what it is. Give it to me." He lunged at Simon, but Simon stepped out of the way. Unfortunately, Simon bumped into the wall and dropped it. The model fell to the floor at the exact wrong angle, and then SNAP, one of its arms broke off.

Alex cried out, then grabbed at Simon's shoulder, shoving him out into the hallway.

"Be careful!" Stella warned, chasing after them.

She wasn't sure exactly what happened next except that the boys tripped and fell and then . . .

Simon was screaming.

Charlie and Mom raced up from the party. "What's wrong? What happened?"

Simon held up his arm and showed his father a scrape on

his elbow. "I wanted to come up and say hi, but they . . . they hurt me!"

Stella's jaw dropped. There was no way Alex had done that. He'd barely touched him.

"He's lying!" Alex answered. "I didn't hurt him. Not on purpose. He broke my model."

Mom placed herself instinctively between Simon and the twins. She glanced through the doorway and saw the mecha lying on the floor, its arm separated from its torso. She kept her voice low so the party guests couldn't hear. "Alex . . . Stella . . . Go to your rooms."

Just before she reached her door, Stella looked back to see Simon sitting near the top of the stairs. She couldn't be sure, but she thought she'd caught him smiling before switching quickly back to tears. Maybe he was playing it up? Or maybe he'd really been hurt but was pleased to see the twins get what he thought they deserved?

From across the kitchen table, Alex caught Stella's gaze. She realized that he'd been listening more closely to Simon's tale than she had been. She felt glad she wasn't letting Simon get to her. The ghost stories he'd already come up with about Wildwyck had crept into her dreams and kept her up at night. Like many old buildings, the place creaked and bumped and whistled and whined into the wee hours, consistently making Stella wake with a start, wondering what might be staring at her from the shadows.

"I turned the knob," said Simon dramatically, as if his story was part of a game. It was how he always told his stories. If it *was* a game, Stella wasn't sure who was meant to be the winner. "I pushed the door slowly, careful to not make a noise. I didn't want to scare away whoever was humming down there in the dark."

Not this again! she thought.

Simon had first mentioned a mysterious humming about a month ago, a week after moving day. He'd snuck into her room and hid under her sheets so that when she came upstairs, he could pop up and scare her. The way he told it was, he was lying very still when he heard Stella approaching, humming a song. Footsteps creaked on the stairs. The humming got louder — Stella was in the doorway. Floorboards squeaked as she crossed the room and then leaned over the mattress, bringing her face close to his. Simon heard a ragged breathing, like a strangled *Huhhhhhh*, and he knew he'd been caught. She'd decided to scare him too. Her breath rustled the top sheet. He tossed it aside and shouted, *BOOO!*

But there was nobody in the room.

He hopped out of the bed and peered under the mattress to see if Stella was hiding. He checked around the edge of the doorway, but the hallway was empty too.

He found her at the kitchen table, eating breakfast.

Not humming.

When he told Stella what had happened in her bedroom, she was furious. She didn't care so much about the ghost part, because *Really? A ghost?* What made her blood boil was that he'd snuck into her room. It was her private space, and he'd touched her things and messed up her bed. Teary-eyed, she'd complained to her mom about what Simon had done. Mom made Simon promise to not go in Stella's bedroom again without her permission.

Simon had explained that he and Zachary always played tricks on each other, and he thought he could do the same with Stella and Alex, but now he knew better.

Or so he'd said.

"Down the dark stairs, I started to feel scared," Simon continued, his voice hushed.

"You *started* to feel scared?" Alex asked.

Simon ignored him. "The humming was still distant. Feeling my way forward, I found a cord, and when I pulled it, a light came on. The walls were cracked and crumbling and covered in cobwebs."

Mom shook her head. "Simon, this is why we don't want you down there."

"I know, but listen . . . The farther I got from the staircase, the louder the humming grew. It was coming from just around a bend. It sounded like a little kid."

"Yeah, right," said Alex. "You expect us to believe that there's a *little kid* hiding in our basement? Humming?"

"I don't expect anything," Simon answered. "I followed the voice into a new room. I noticed a small wooden door in the far wall, shut tight. It looks ancient. Wide planks and huge rusty nail heads. There isn't even a doorknob. Just a big metal loop bolted to the wood. The door is coated in dust, like something you'd see in a castle filled with vampires."

"Great," Stella mumbled to Alex. "Now it's *vampires*."

Mom shook her head. "Simon — "

"Wait, Bev, there's more!"

"There's always more," said Alex.

"*Alex*," Mom warned.

Simon barreled onward anyway. "The humming stopped. I asked, *Who's there?* No answer. So I grabbed the rusted loop. The door wouldn't budge. Bev, do you know if it's bolted from the other side?"

"I'm not even sure which door you mean."

"All of a sudden . . ." Simon slapped his palm against the table. "*BAM!*" Everyone flinched. Stella clasped her notebook, angry at herself for giving Simon what he wanted. "Something pounded from inside. I don't even how to describe what I heard next. It was like a scream mixed with a howl and a sob. It didn't sound human, but also, like, it wasn't an animal? Next, there came a growling sound. It got so loud, I tripped backward. Almost fell. And that was *before* the door started rattling! I was so scared I couldn't move. But then . . ." Simon looked around the table, meeting each of their stares. "It just stopped. I ran. Around the corner. Down the hall. Up the stairs. I ran until I found Stella in the kitchen. And I told her what I heard."

"You told me it was a ghost," Stella answered quietly. "That doesn't sound like a ghost."

"What does it sound like?" Simon asked.

"Werewolves," Alex answered flatly. "Mom, call an exterminator."

"Funny, Alex," Mom sighed, then stood. "How about you three head outside for a bit?

Simon scowled. "I didn't finish the story."

"I think we get your point." She waved him away, like a bug. "Now go get some fresh air."

"Mom," Stella whispered harshly. She thought she'd made herself clear about hanging out with Simon. Mom gave Stella a look that said, *Help me out, please.* Her Bowie concert T-shirt was torn at the shoulder and spattered with paint. Her brown pixie cut was sticking up all over, but not on purpose and not in a cute way. Until recently, she and Stella had shared a similar ponytail, but with all the sweat and grime of restoring the building, Mom had chopped it off to keep it from sticking to her neck. Stella had felt bad about the change at first. She liked looking just like her mother. But they still had the same milky Polish skin, the same blue eyes, the same apple-plump cheeks, and the same deep hair color, which Stella figured was good enough for now. Her mother was only trying her best. Stella wanted to try her best too. With a soft smile, she lifted the cracked bowl from the sink and tossed the pieces into the garbage.

"Charlie should be home by the time you get back," Mom said. "I'll make us lunch."

"No soup," said Simon. "I hate soup."

"It's a little hot for soup," Mom answered. "How about chicken salad?"

"No raisins," said Simon. "I hate raisins."

"Who puts raisins in chicken salad?" Alex asked with a sneer.

"My mom does," said Simon. "All the time. It's really good, actually."

"Didn't you just say you hated raisins?"

"They're good in chicken salad, but only when *my* mom puts them in."

Stella looked at Alex and rolled her eyes.

"Okay, then!" Mom clapped. "Everyone out. Have fun!"

As if that were possible, Stella thought as she glanced nervously at the basement door before following the boys outside.

CHAPTER TWO
ALEX

"WHICH WAY SHOULD we go?" Simon asked, running through the courtyard ahead of the twins.

Alex felt himself tense. How could Simon act as if everything was fine, as if he hadn't just made a huge scene about encountering a howling, growling, humming ghost locked behind a mysterious door in the basement? Stella must have sensed his annoyance, because when she touched Alex's elbow and caught his attention, she was wearing her *calm-down* expression. Her eyebrows spoke volumes.

"Let's go check out the old barn," she suggested. "I still think I might be able to convince Mom to let us set up a horse stable there if I fix it up."

Simon laughed. "Yeah, right. Bev's never going to let you get a horse."

Stella shrugged. "That's fine. I don't want *a* horse. I want three!" This made Simon chortle harder.

Alex bristled. "The barn it is."

"Maybe it's haunted too!" said Simon.

"What's with you and all these stories?" Alex asked, trudging through the tall grass past the corner of the house's north wing. "Do you think it's fun to try to scare us? Or do you really believe there's a ghost here at Wildwyck?"

"Just because you don't believe it doesn't mean it's not true."

"Just because you keep telling the stories doesn't mean they *are* true!"

"I'm trying to help," said Simon.

"Help how?" Alex asked.

"By warning about the scary things that could come get you and Stella in the middle of the night. It's best to be prepared."

"We're supposed to fight a ghost?"

"You don't fight ghosts!" Simon yelled.

"Okay, then, what *do* you do with them?" Stella asked as politely as possible.

"You make friends."

"And what if they don't want to be friends with you?" Alex answered. "What then?"

"You keep trying," said Simon.

Alex scoffed. "Because you're *so* good at friend-making."

Simon skipped ahead. "If I can't make friends with the ghost, then my mom will just have to let me go back and live with her in Ohio. I'd be fine with that."

Alex sighed. This wasn't the first time Simon had mentioned wanting to live with his mother. Alex was pretty sure it was one of the reasons that he'd been acting up. If he made himself annoying enough, maybe his dad would want to get rid of him. "Have you ever considered that your mom doesn't *want* you back in Ohio?"

"Alex!" Stella yelped in surprise.

"I'm gonna tell Zachary you just said that." Simon squinted.

"And what's Zachary going to do about it?" Alex wouldn't

back down, especially not now that Simon had mentioned his older brother. Alex and Zachary had always gotten along.

"The barn is just ahead," said Stella. "Whoa, Simon. You're right. It does look pretty spooky." This made Simon smile. Forgetting the argument, he took off toward the barn, leaving Alex and Stella alone for a moment in the tall grass.

"Smooth," Alex whispered.

"It's better if we all try to get along."

Alex shook his head. "What happened to wanting nothing to do with him?"

"I don't know. It's just . . . exhausting . . . fighting all the time. Can you please be nice for a while? For me?" Stella shifted from one foot to the other, her eyes pleading.

Alex sniffed. Then he grinned. "For you, Sis? Anything."

The red barn stood farther up the slight slope, across a wide field from the house, at the juncture of the trees and an ancient-looking stone wall that snaked into the woods.

Alex and Stella had been lucky, living so close to Prospect Park in Brooklyn. It was one of the only places in the city where you could walk and not feel like you were surrounded entirely by high-rise apartment buildings. Alex had loved walking there with his dad. On certain trails, it was like they weren't in a city at all. The woods in Brooklyn didn't compare with what you'd find here in the mountains though. Some of these trees were giants, like creatures out of a science-fiction story about alien dimensions. He wished his dad could have seen them. Some grew so high, they made Alex feel tiny — tinier even than he usually felt. Even though they were twins, Stella was already taller than him by an inch. Thank goodness he had some height on Simon. Still, when he stared up at the leaves around here, he had the sensation sometimes that he was *shrinking-shrinking-shrinking* down to nothing. It made him sad. As sad as he'd been to leave Brooklyn and all his friends and neighbors, classmates, and teachers. As sad as when his dad . . . Well, maybe not *that* sad. Dr. Solomon told him he had to do it though, to leave, so that his mom would be happy again.

So that the family could heal.

Not everything is about you, Alex.

Mom had reconnected with Charlie over Facebook about a year after the twins' father had passed away. Charlie was still living in Ohio back then. When Mom had mentioned that she was dating a man so far away, the twins were angry and confused. But then they saw how happy Mom was whenever she video-chatted with Charlie, how she seemed to be coming back to life after the *very dark time.* They decided to be happy for her too, if only because they'd been finding it difficult to be happy for themselves. They missed Dad more than words could express. More than stars missed the moon on the blackest of nights. Walking the streets where the accident had happened only made the pain grow larger. So maybe it was better that they were all moving on.

Mom's background was in interior design, and Charlie was in construction. He'd been wanting to break out on his own for a while, and Mom thought it was time to escape Brooklyn, so they'd begun looking for a place between their cities, a property that would allow them to combine their interests.

When they discovered a listing for a boys' school in disrepair in the foothills of the Catskill Mountains, they knew they had to check it out. Mom had come home to Brooklyn raving to the twins about all the possibilities. And after Alex saw pictures of the area, he was thrilled. He loved models of architecture and early airplanes and the first cars and military boats, some of which, he'd learned, had been constructed in ports along the Hudson River.

Charlie's plan had been to acquire the property and then live with the family in the center section of the main house while he and Mom converted the other wings into town houses. It was a good investment, Charlie promised. Mom was certain other New Yorkers would want to make their way out to the country as well. *Who knows?* she'd said shortly after making the decision official. *Maybe one of Alex's or Stella's city friends would end up being their country neighbors.*

What no one had counted on was chaos in the form of a ten-year-old stepbrother.

"I beat you!" Simon called out from the front of the barn.

Stella was halfway between the two boys. Alex, lost in thought, had been trailing behind.

"You sure did," said Stella. "Good job."

"What should we do now?" Simon asked, looking bored already.

It was amazing to Alex how quickly the kid was able to switch between anger and excitement, joy and fear, kindness and pure evil. Alex tried to recognize himself in Simon, in

any small part, but he just couldn't do it. Simon's hair was
blond, short, and stiff while Alex's was a thick brown mop.
Simon's eyes were dark, like oceans, while Alex's were blue,
like skies. Simon's nose was thick, like nerdy boys in car-
toons. Alex's was pointy and curved slightly to the left. But
all that stuff was on the outside. Inside, where it really mat-
tered, their differences couldn't even be counted.

"You can help me clean up," Stella suggested. "We'll stack
the old wood and . . ." Simon made a face. "You have a better
idea?"

"Let's play your racing game!"

Alex perked up. Since the move, he and Stella had been
timing each other, running around all three wings of the
house. It was like the routine they used to do with Dad in
the evenings, after he was home from work, when they'd loop
around the block in Brooklyn. Even though the barn wasn't as
wide as the house, it might be enough to exhaust Simon a bit.
Alex took out the phone he shared with his sister. "Sounds
good to me." He opened the timer. "I'll count you down from
five. Finish line is right where you started. Okay?"

"Okay!" Simon cheered.

Alex held his thumb over the button. "Five. Four. Three.
Two. One!"

Simon took off at a sprint, running across where the barn's
broken doors yawned wide.

Once he had disappeared around the corner, Stella gave
Alex's shoulder a soft punch. "See?" she said. "Not so hard to
be kind."

"Tell that to Simon," Alex said, chuckling. "At least he's out of our hair for the next few seconds."

"*Out of Our Hair!*" Stella exclaimed. "That's a good one for the list."

Smiling, Alex pulled up the Notes app on their phone. "I like it," he said, typing it into the document. For years, the twins had been recording words and phrases that they thought would be good titles for things. Songs. Books. Poems. Bands. TV shows. It had been a game that their father had started with them when they were young. Only recently had Alex migrated the list onto the phone, so he wouldn't have to carry around his dad's old notebook and risk losing it. Even though Stella's ideas kept to a common theme — *Dream Horse*, *Fire Horse*, *Tiny Horse* — he always included them so she wouldn't feel left out, but he liked his ideas better. *Tossed and Turned*, *The Beaten Path*, and *Beware Mermaids* — a phrase he'd seen a few weeks ago on a sign posted at a lighthouse out on the Hudson.

"Where's Simon?" Stella asked. "He should've been back by now."

Alex felt his face flush. "Ugh," he groaned. "He's messing with us already?"

"Let's go find the little creeper."

CHAPTER THREE
ALEX

THEY WENT AROUND the barn the opposite way. When they passed the far corner and didn't see Simon, Alex started to worry. Had the kid managed to hurt himself?

Or was this another trick?

"Simon!" Stella called out, sounding worried.

"Don't give him what he wants," Alex chided. But when the late-summer cry of crickets made him turn to the dark woods, something inside him shriveled. The dense trees. The mountains. The wild rivers, and even sometimes the wind through Wildwyck's eaves at night. It all often seemed like too much. He hadn't told anyone how nervous he was to begin at Frost Meadow Middle School, not even Stella. He worried that his fears were why Simon had been getting to him so much lately, and why the stories of ghosts at Wildwyck seemed to stab deeper than they normally would. Everything about moving here without Dad had been hard, but the hardest part, he was sure now, was pretending that it had been easy.

The barn towered overhead, seeming almost to lean, as if one big gust would send it crashing over them, a red wave made of splinters. Though the sun was still climbing toward its midday high point, and the air was getting hot enough to bake dirt, there came a coolness from up the slope. Not quite a breeze. The grass tickled Alex's calves as he followed Stella farther around the back side of the structure.

As Alex approached the edge of the barn, he was suddenly concerned that Simon would leap out at them. Make them shout. He grabbed at Stella's arm to stop her, but she pulled away, her attention already fixed on the old stone wall. "What do you see?" he asked.

"Simon?" Stella called again, this time softly.

A shadowy figure was standing beside the wall a dozen feet past the line of trees, hidden inside the dim canopy. When Stella's Converse sneakers came down on a brittle stick, the figure turned. A beam of sunlight drifted through the branches and struck the exact right spot so that Simon's face was revealed, like a magic trick on a stage. His eyes were round with awe.

Stella stomped her foot. "We were waiting for you! Why didn't you answer us?"

"Shh," he answered, turning back to the woods. "There's . . . something in there."

"*Something?*" Alex echoed. "Something like what? A dog? A bear? A large man with an axe?"

Simon waved them up the path, then stepped farther into the shadows. "A little girl. I didn't want to scare her off. I think . . . I think she was the ghost I heard humming in the basement."

Alex stopped short and turned to his sister. "I'm not falling for this again."

Stella held up her hands. "What are we going to do? Let him wander into the woods alone?"

"When did he suddenly become *our* responsibility? He's only like a year and a half younger than us. He's no baby."

"Oh wow!" Simon was about to disappear over the crest of the hill. "You two have to come see this!"

Alex half stumbled, half jogged the dozen or so yards along the path. Ahead, Stella planted her feet and stared. "What is it?" he whispered, but by then he could see the grassy clearing. "Are those graves?"

Simon was already strolling among the monuments. Stella took off running. Alex made his way down the path more slowly than the others. His chest felt tight. He couldn't stop thinking about what Simon had said while standing next to the stone wall. *A little girl . . . I think she was the ghost . . .*

In the clearing, a spot of sun shone down on the stones, which seemed to almost glow. Alex glanced around. Was there actually a little girl out here? Could she be a neighbor?

"Whoa," Simon whispered, crouching and staring at the deep etchings in the stone. "This must be the Wildwyck family plot."

"What's a *family plot*?" Stella asked, wandering nearer.

"Look at the dates . . . These go back over a hundred years!"

That got Alex's attention. Did Charlie know about this? Maybe there was some information hidden away in the house, records he might be able to scour, to learn about this family. He checked out a dark gray stone with a bluish hue. Pieces around the edges had chipped off, but it was in extraordinary condition for being almost two hundred years old. "Jonas Wildwyck. Born 1770. Died 1835."

Simon rushed over. "That's even earlier than the ones I found." He ran his fingers over the carvings, as if that would tell him more about the person buried there. "If this is the oldest grave, maybe this Jonas guy was the one who built our house. Maybe he's the one who made that old locked door in the basement."

"Oh, how sad!" Stella exclaimed, leaning over a patch of ground a dozen feet away. Alex was pretty sure she'd interrupted Simon on purpose. "This one belongs to a girl . . . Wow, she was just about my age."

Simon's face lit up. "Really?" It was creepy how excited he looked. He darted over to see the grave, practically pushing Stella out of the way. Brushing away dead grass, he read, "Margaret Wildwyck. 1963 to 1975." He glanced up at the twins. "That would make her — "

"Twelve years old," said Alex. "When she died."

"I wonder what happened to her?" Stella asked.

"Maybe she was murdered," Alex teased, trying to give back to Simon what he'd been giving them all summer.

"Don't say that," Stella scolded. "She was a real person." Alex felt his face flush. He hadn't meant to be disrespectful. Stella stared at the grass under her feet. She brought her voice low and then added, "She still is. Down there. Margaret Wildwyck."

"Shh," Simon said. He glanced around the clearing, his eyes wide. Searching. "Do you hear that?"

Alex took his sister's hand. All he could hear were crickets and a soft breeze rustling the leaves overhead.

"What is it?" Stella asked.

Alex squeezed her fingers. He didn't want her falling for another of Simon's tricks. She pulled her hand away, and Alex clicked his tongue in frustration.

"It's the humming from this morning." Simon continued to peer into the shadows.

Alex didn't hear anything. And from the look on Stella's face, he didn't think she did either.

A little girl . . . I think she was the ghost . . .

Alex couldn't believe Simon was trying this again. "Come on," he said to Stella. "Let's go back to the house. Mom's probably waiting with the chicken salad." He glared down at Simon. "*Without raisins.*"

"No, wait!" Simon cried out. He leaned closer to Margaret's marker. "It's coming from . . . from the stone . . ."

"Oh, stop it!" Stella begged. "Don't be grotesque." Alex raised an eyebrow, impressed by his sister's vocabulary, but she frowned, unamused.

Simon sat back on his heels. He closed his eyes, then *he* began to hum. It wasn't a tune that Alex had ever heard before, but it felt familiar. Slow and plodding, like a church hymn.

A hymn . . .

Organ music sounded in Alex's memory. A crowd of people filled his mind. All dressed in black. Spilling out of the small chapel onto Sixth Avenue in Park Slope . . .

"Let's go," Alex said. The words felt like sand in his mouth. Baked and dusty.

Simon only hummed louder. He began to rock forward and back, leaning over the gravestone. Forward and back. Forward and back.

"Simon?" Stella tried. "Are you all right?"

Alex shot her a *why-bother* look. But Stella seemed truly concerned.

Simon's rocking grew almost violent. Forward and back. Forward and back. Stella reached for his shoulder, but Simon knocked her hand away. He quit humming and was now whispering, as if talking to the stone. Alex couldn't make out any of what his stepbrother was saying. Maybe it was all nonsense.

Or maybe . . .

"Let's go," Alex yelled to his sister. Stella flinched, then nodded. "Simon. We're leaving. If you don't get up right now, you're going to be here all alone."

Simon clasped his hands in front of his chest. He bent toward the girl's grave, his forehead nearly touching the ground. His whispering was intense, but Alex still could not make out what he was saying.

Was he talking to the girl?

Was *she* talking *through* him?

A little girl . . . I think she was the ghost . . .

Chapter Four
Stella

"You left him *where*?" Mom's jaw dropped in disbelief.

"There's a small graveyard in the forest," Stella explained.

Mom shuddered. "No, sweetie, I heard that part. I just . . . I'm having a hard time believing that you two left a ten-year-old by himself. In the woods."

Coming back to the house, they'd found that she'd laid out a picnic blanket on the grass in the courtyard. There was a pile of paper plates and napkins. A stack of bread slices. A Pyrex bowl filled with her freshly made chicken salad, covered with plastic to protect it from the flies.

"He's ten and a half," Stella murmured.

Mom puffed out her cheeks and ran her fingers through her short hair.

"He was being a jerk!" Alex insisted. "He was acting all, I don't know, possessed."

"Possessed? What does that even mean?"

"He was doing the ghost thing again. He said he'd seen a strange girl up there."

Mom's eyes only grew wider. "And you left him. Alone. In a graveyard."

Charlie stepped out the front door and onto the steps. "Simon is *where*?"

And just like that, the four of them were heading back across the field toward the barn.

Stella's face felt sunburned, but she knew that warmth was also coming from inside her. Anger. Guilt. And in the center of it all floated Simon's smug little face, grinning, just like at the Christmas party when he'd gotten the twins in trouble. Stella and Alex both knew that one of Simon's most impressive talents was playing the victim. *What might the results be this time?* she wondered. *More tears? A tantrum? Or would he pull something even more drastic?*

"Simon!" Charlie bellowed, even though they were only halfway there.

Stella imagined Simon marching out from around the barn, looking confused. Or amused. Would Charlie apologize then for making such a fuss? Would Mom?

"You two have got to do better with Simon," Charlie said, glancing back. "He looks up to you."

"He looks up to *Zachary*," Alex muttered.

Mom threw him a look of annoyance.

Alex whispered to Stella, "They know it's true."

"Sorry, Charlie," Stella forced herself to answer. "It's just . . . He was trying to scare me again."

Charlie sniffed. "I'd think, at your age, Stella, you wouldn't let a kid have that power over you."

"Did either of you see the girl Simon mentioned?" Mom asked.

"Nope," Stella said, and directed this next part at her stepfather. "Simon made her up. Just like he made up hearing that humming down in the basement this morning."

Mom sighed. Charlie paused. "He was down in the base-ment again?"

"I was going to mention it," Mom answered quietly.

"He just doesn't listen."

Stella grinned at Alex. He smirked.

On their right, the stone wall edged up to the path. The barn was ahead to their left. And straight on stood the shad-owed opening into the woods.

Stella didn't like cemeteries. The idea of all those cof-fins just under the surface, hidden by a soft blanket of green. The forced beauty, manicured lawns, flowers both real and plastic — it all seemed like a lie. One of the hardest parts of moving was being so far away from her father. It wasn't that Stella wanted so badly to go back and sit by his grave, but before the move, it was a comfort knowing how close he was. Now it was a two-and-a-half-hour drive. She could already feel him starting to slip from her memories. She almost wished she believed in ghosts.

She liked Charlie — liked him for her mother. Liked the guy he was. Generous. Gentle. Patient. For the most part. Today was the first time she'd seen Charlie look truly upset at them. And of course, *of course*, it was Simon who'd made that happen.

At the edge of the woods, Charlie and Mom stopped and stared, as if they sensed something strange about the shadows.

"The graveyard is over the hill." Alex nudged at them.

A moment passed before they continued onward. Stella followed her mother, who followed Charlie. Alex rounded up the rear. Stella felt an almost giddy joy, imagining all the ways Charlie might scold Simon.

Ahead, Charlie and Mom stopped, blocking the way.

Stella scooted past them to find that, except for the fading sunbeam, the graveyard was empty.

"Simon!" Charlie bellowed again.

Mom took the path quickly, moving through the gravestones. "Simon, honey?" she tried, her voice wavering. Charlie clomped down after her.

Stella stood with Alex at the top of the hill. People often asked the twins if they could read each other's minds. Stella had always scoffed, but the truth was, there were times when she did sense her brother's thoughts. Like now.

He's faking.

He's hiding.

No way. He wouldn't do that to his father.

Maybe he would . . .

He's in trouble. Someone took him.

A girl . . . Maybe she was the ghost . . .

Stella felt her lungs clench. Her skin tingled and a choke rose up her esophagus. She bit her lip to keep back tears. She glanced at Alex. He was doing the same.

After they'd scoured the clearing for any sign of Simon — footprints, a piece of his clothing, a smear of mud, or a mark on a tree trunk — Charlie and Bev searched the woods beyond, calling his name, again and again. Stella and Alex waited among the gravestones, not speaking. If Simon was really gone, would Mom blame the twins?

Stella stiffened. Excuses bloomed but then wilted. The truth felt poisonous.

"What do we do?" Alex whispered.

"We stay here. Until he comes back. Or until Mom and Charlie come back. Or until . . ."

Stella's ankle rolled as she shifted her weight. She looked down and realized she'd been standing on a gravestone. Margaret Wildwyck. The one who'd started all this.

Stella wondered how she had died. A tractor accident? Or maybe she'd fallen off a horse . . . Had she been swallowed up by a sinkhole? Or quicksand! The possibilities seemed endless. Stella's mom had been born back around when Margaret died, and she'd shared tons of stories about how things had been different. Parents hadn't watched their kids as closely. Strangers had driven around in white vans, dressed as clowns, randomly snatching up children. She stared down at the etched words. The name. The dates.

For a moment, Stella felt strange. The fringes of her vision went dark, and the stone reflected a face back up at her. A face that didn't belong to her. A melody crept into her mind. It was the one that Simon had been warbling earlier. The one he'd said had belonged to the ghost girl.

But who was singing it now?

A voice. Breath against her earlobe.

Before she knew it, Stella had dropped to her knees. Her chin bounced off her sternum. She was about to fall face-first onto the ground when hands caught her shoulders.

"What happened?"

"I don't know . . ." she heard herself answer. Alex was crouching beside her, looking worried. "I want to go home."

"Come on." He stood, trying to lift her. "I'll take you."

"No." Stella pulled away, still wobbly. She caught herself, pressing a palm into the grass. "To our *real* home." When Alex wrapped his arms around her, she began to cry. She felt weak and angry. This only made her heave with sobs, just as — she imagined — Simon would have wanted.

CHAPTER FIVE
ZACHARY

August 17

These have been some strange days. I blame my little brother.

Simon is a pretty sensitive kid, which is one of the reasons we share the attic bedroom here at Wildwyck. It's the biggest room in the house, so we have plenty of space to ourselves, but Simon doesn't like to be alone, not at night. Even though he says he's into scary movies and ghost stories and stuff like that, they get to him more than he'll admit. He's tried to crawl into bed with me a couple times since the move to Frost Meadow, but I keep telling him he needs to grow up. He can be a lot to deal with, as the new members of our family have been learning. And today was one of the strangest we've had yet.

It started off ordinarily enough. I went into the village to hang out with these kids I met at freshman orientation last week — this guy Joshua and this girl Peggy and also some of their friends who I don't really know yet. In the park, there was an actual skate area, with ramps and rails and a half-pipe and everything, which I thought was weird and cool because Frost Meadow is basically Podunk and who would have thought they'd let kids skate here. I was kind of embarrassed because I had to admit I've never done it before, but Joshua was cool. He let me try his board, and I only fell twice, which, let me tell you, is a big deal, because IT IS DIFFICULT. Eventually, they all had to leave, so I get home and find Dad and Bev and the twins freaking out in the courtyard.

My first thought is SIMON.

Sure enough, Dad tells me he's MISSING.

Bev wants to call the police, but Dad says we still need to search the house and the shed. I could tell that Dad was mad at Alex and Stella, so I pulled them aside and asked what was really going on, and they tell me this nutty story about ghosts, and noises in the house, and Simon going to the basement where he wasn't supposed to be and how he'd heard this growling sound from behind an old locked door down there. Later, the three of them found an old graveyard out in the woods!

They'd gotten separated and now Simon was nowhere to be seen. But I KNEW he was messing with them.

I convince everyone to come inside and I say really loudly, NO DAD, DON'T INVOLVE THE POLICE! And before I could blink, Simon comes strolling into the kitchen dragging a blanket he'd pulled off the couch in the den.

Everyone stares at him, like they couldn't believe what they were seeing. And he goes: What's wrong? And then he yawns. The faker! Sometimes I want to kick him.

Unfortunately, Bev didn't see through his act. She runs over and hugs him and asks, Couldn't you hear us calling for you?

And Simon says, After Alex and Stella left me in the woods, I was so tired, I came back here and fell asleep in the den. Finished with his trademark taunt: <u>Sor-ry</u>. And he's looking at Alex and Stella like he's <u>stabbing</u> them with the word.

Dad didn't want to scold the twins any more than he'd already done. But he knew he couldn't leave everything like this, so he let Bev handle them, and asked me and Simon to follow him up to our room in the attic. He sat us down. Honestly, I wasn't sure why I was there, since none of this had to do with me.

But Dad says to us: You have to be more careful with the twins. Simon blinked, as if he had no idea what Dad was talking about. So Dad goes on, The ghost stories have to stop, Simon.

Simon answers, But I saw what I saw. I just wanted everyone to know.

Dad is like, We <u>know</u> what you wanted everyone to know. But all this talk about spirits and hauntings... It's insensitive, Simon. Those kids lost their father and they're struggling with what that means. How they'll live their lives without him. How you and me and Zachary factor into everything now.

What you've been doing is hurtful, he says. I know you're better than that. Then he looked to me and added, Can't you try and be a little more like your big brother?

I had to keep myself from rolling my eyes, because, like, really, Dad?

Simon tears up. All he says is, I miss Mom. He didn't even respond about the twins. But that's Simon — always thinking about himself. Dad sighs, and gives us both hugs, and then goes downstairs.

That's when I notice Simon smiling.

I ask, Are you going to tell me what really happened?

Turns out, he'd watched from the other side of the stone wall as they'd come over the hill, calling his name.

They deserved it, he says. They wouldn't believe me about the girl. They didn't listen about the humming. Or about the door in the basement. Served them right for leaving.

Simon hates when people don't believe him. Even when he's not telling the truth.

He's mentioned a few times that he's sure the twins don't like him. He keeps bringing up that first visit to Brooklyn, when they'd been kind of cold. I've tried to explain that it must have been a scary time for everyone, and that meeting Dad maybe wasn't the way the twins had expected to spend their winter break. Simon says he knew that what he'd done was wrong, breaking Alex's model, getting them in trouble like that. But seeing the looks on their faces when he faked those tears, when Bev had scolded them, and then afterward, when he'd smiled, letting Stella know not to mess with him . . . He said it felt good.

How am I supposed to respond to that?

He says, The game isn't over yet.

And I say, Maybe it should be.

What's the worst that could happen, he asks. Dad and Bev might send me back to Ohio? I never wanted to come here in the first place!

That morning, he'd yelled at Stella, There's a ghost in the basement! I wanted to know which parts of _that_ story were true.

He said it was true that he'd followed the humming to the basement in the morning and that he'd discovered an old door. But had there been a growling sound behind it? He said he could hear it in his memory. Pain and fear and warning. But was he remembering only what he'd imagined? Was his imagination making the memory less true?

Me and Simon have known about the graveyard since coming to Wildwyck. We've gone up several times already. It was a secret spot. A spooky spot.

Simon says he's surprised how little it took to get Alex and Stella going: him pausing behind the barn during what was supposed to be his sprint, waiting for them up the path, inventing the story of seeing a girl, knowing that he'd show them the grave he'd stumbled upon weeks earlier, the one that belonged to that girl who died back in the 1970s. Maybe she really is haunting the house, Simon says. Maybe she is the one who was humming. But that isn't the point.

I ask, What is the point, then?

Simon laughs. He says, To make them believe it. And this part stuck with me. He goes: Everyone knows that one of the best ways to get people to listen to you, to actually see you, and hear you, is to scare them.

When we moved in, there were flies in the attic. Dad hung sticky strips from the ceiling to catch them. They worked like charms. Whenever a fly landed on the strip, the glue would hold it tight.

The thing about these kinds of traps is, the flies hold on for days. Whenever I checked how many more had been caught, if I bumped a strip, even the ones that had been there the longest seemed to come to life, as if I'd reminded them, gave them hope that they should keep fighting, keep buzzing, keep making noise.

Now thinking about Simon's ghost stories, the ones he's told since we've moved in, I can't help imagining the flies stuck on those strips. What does it take to stir up a spirit that's been quiet, waiting for rescue or a kind of release? Could our family's coming here have been like when I touched the traps? Only the flies are ghosts, and our house is like the glue?

At night in my bed by the window, listening to the sounds outside, it almost seems possible.

That's the thing about strange days. Isn't it? Once they arrive, they only seem to get stranger.

I'm not sure what to believe anymore, especially if it comes out of Simon's mouth. I'll have to ask Joshua and Peggy the next time we all hang out if anyone has ever seen ghosts at Wildwyck and if I should be worried.

Your friend,

Zachary Kidd

CHAPTER SIX
SIMON

THAT NIGHT, SIMON woke with a full bladder, so he got out of bed and went down to the hallway below. He paused before Alex's open door and listened to his stepbrother breathing deeply as he slept. Next door, Stella was completely silent.

The day had not gone how he'd meant it to. The twins probably thought he was a monster. Part of him wanted to not care, but how could you not care when your family thought you were monstrous?

He flicked the light switch in the bathroom and closed the door. He still wasn't used to this setup. Back in Ohio, the bathroom had always been just outside his bedroom. But here, getting to it was almost like navigating a labyrinth.

Simon had always loved scary things. When he was younger, Zachary would tell him stories about vampires and zombies and witches and mad scientists. If ever there was an afternoon when their mother wasn't paying close attention, they'd watch spooky YouTube clips and TV shows on Zachary's computer. They'd even set up a secret spot in the basement crawl space behind the oil tank in the Ohio house, where they'd laid out blankets and pillows and a little table where Zachary would light a candle and they'd attempt to conjure up spirits. "Are you trying to burn the house down?" Mom had yelled when she'd discovered it. Simon had thought it was funny that she was angrier about fire than she was about them making the house haunted.

Soon Simon was looking everywhere for ghosts. Sometimes he was certain he could see them from the corners of his eyes, but when he'd look again, there'd be nothing there. At night, he'd listen to every creak that came out of the quiet, wondering who, or what, might be coming his way. He'd duck under his covers, sometimes staying awake till sunrise, his imagination whirling with images of tattered sheets flickering in the wind, black top hats floating up dusty staircases, pale faces jolting out from darkness, flesh oozing and skin slipping off bone. Of course, his mother didn't like him talking about what he saw, or at least what he imagined he *might* see. So he made sure to only tell the other kids in the neighborhood whenever the grown-ups weren't around. If he mentioned his ghosts to Zachary, his older brother would just laugh. Simon wasn't sure if that meant Zachary thought he was being funny, or if he thought he was being ridiculous.

It felt odd to Simon, growing up with a sibling who was three years older. Zachary was constantly changing — what he liked, *who* he liked, how much time he was willing to spend with you, and just when you thought you'd caught up, *could* keep up, he would go and change again.

Simon had felt strange the moment his father had pulled the pickup into Wildwyck's driveway. The sensation was like a shift in the light that comes with a new season. In the foyer of the main wing, the feeling swooped upon him, stronger than it had ever been, and he understood. Something was here. Something that wasn't quite . . . *normal*. It was the first time since Dad had told him they'd be moving to New York with Bev's kids that Simon felt actually excited about the changes that were happening to his family.

The new house was massive. Supposedly, the building had once been a school for troubled boys. Back in Ohio, Zachary had looked it up and told him that the students had come from all over, but mostly from New York City. "Just like the twins," Simon had said with a laugh. "Troubled *and* from New York." It stood three stories tall. Two wings reached out like arms from either side of the main hall, most of the windows still boarded up. The steeply slanted slate roof connected all three sections of the building. Evenly spaced windows provided views of the surrounding pastures and trees, the barn, and the abandoned, crumbling bridge that crossed a meandering creek.

Wildwyck was a dream come true, but now he had to live with the twins. Often, he didn't know how to talk to them, in case he said something accidently hurtful about not having their dad around anymore. The easiest thing to do was what he and Zachary had done ever since he could remember: Play games. Tease. Set up elaborate pranks. That's what the tale of the house growling and the ghost girl humming and the graveyard in the woods had been all about today. He hadn't meant to make Stella cry. Of course, now no one believed him about that, just like how they refused to believe him about the strange things he'd seen and felt around Wildwyck. Both Dad and Zachary had scolded him, which only made him *not* want to apologize to the twins. Alex and Stella had never apologized to him for the things that they did: Ignoring him. Making him feel invisible. Making him feel like he knew nothing compared to them. It was rude. Ruder than anything he could come up with to get them back. So why was HE the one everyone thought was the villain?

He pushed the toilet handle, and the water ran in the bowl. He washed his hands quickly and then wiped them on his pajamas. Opening the door again, a girl was standing in the hall in the dark. Simon nearly yelped but then caught sight of Stella's face. She didn't look happy.

"What you did today was not okay," she whispered.

Now he was supposed to apologize, wasn't he? "It was just a joke, Stella."

She blocked his way. "Do you like scaring people?"

"Yes, actually."

"Well . . . I don't like being scared. You really freaked us out. How would you like it if me and Alex tried to scare you?"

Again, this way she had of talking down to him. Like he was a baby. Annoyance burbled inside him. "I might love it."

Stella sighed, letting down her guard. "We don't like fighting with you, Simon."

"I feel like sometimes Alex does."

"My brother is having a harder time with all this than the rest of us. He misses talking with Dr. Solomon, our counselor. She was a big help after Dad . . . Well, I guess I'm saying, just give him a break. Okay? That's the only way things are going to get better. For all of us."

Simon knew he should say yes, okay, I'm sorry. But why had no one offered to give him a break too? No, he hadn't lost a parent. But in a way . . . hadn't he? Why hadn't anyone offered *him* a counselor? Not that he would have gone, but still . . .

The best he could do for Stella was "I'll try." When she stared at him, unmoving, squinting in the light from the bathroom, he went on, "You need the toilet?"

Stella rolled her eyes and turned to her room, sliding back into the shadows.

CHAPTER SEVEN
STELLA

THE BUS WAS zooming along the rough county route, up and down hills, veering sharply around curves, when it hit a bump. Stella's pencil skidded off her notebook's page, leaving a deep, dark line. "Shoot," she whispered, rubbing away the mark as best she could.

Beside her, Alex was wearing his headphones. He leaned close. "What happened?"

Stella sighed. She'd been happy with this new drawing. Two unicorns at a table playing chess. Now it was ruined. "I messed up."

Simon poked up his head from the seat in front of them. "Messed up *what*?"

Stella forced herself to answer him. "My drawing." She closed her notebook before he could get a proper glance. Ever since the day, two weeks prior, when he'd caused all that trouble, she was keeping her distance. Alex was too.

Simon frowned and then slid back down in his seat.

There were only a handful of other kids on the bus, and most of them were keeping to themselves, which was fine with Stella. It was the twins' first day of sixth grade, and Simon's first day of fifth. If they were still back in Brooklyn, there wouldn't be an issue, because Simon would be going to a separate school. But here, in Frost Meadow, students started middle school early — hence, the three were riding the same bus to the same building.

Stella closed her eyes and breathed deeply. She wasn't sure she was ready for this change. She'd woken before sunrise. Crisp air coming through the window gave her a feeling almost of ice in the lungs. It always showed up around this time. Usually, it made her buzz, excited for what was new. This year, it had brought tears, and she couldn't say why. Her mother had made scrambled eggs and toast, but Stella hadn't been able to take more than two bites before feeling full. Feeling *ill*. She'd kept that to herself. She didn't want her mom thinking she was acting like a baby.

Every first day of school since Dad had died had been like icicles through her brain. This one was shaping up to be the same.

The town of Frost Meadow appeared before them. Quaint little houses lined the street. They almost didn't look real, like something you'd see in a movie or on a postcard from a place you might only ever visit. As the bus crossed a short, red, steel bridge over a creek, Stella looked out the window and watched the water spill over a rock ledge and disappear into the woods. The bus slowed, then pulled into a circular drive before a wide, two-story brick building.

As everyone stood, Stella had to grab onto the back of the seat to steady herself. Maybe she should've tried to eat a bit more before leaving the house, because now she felt wobbly. Her heart galloped as she stepped down off the bus. She kept her twin in the corner of her vision, which helped her feel a little less nervous, as they both made their way up the front walk to the main entrance.

A week ago, Mom had brought them to meet the principal, Mrs. Hitchens, and their guidance counselor, Mr. Kuchelmann. They seemed nice enough. Mrs. Hitchens and Mr. Kuchelmann had shown them around. Cinder block walls. Blue linoleum floors. The lingering smell of disinfectant. It wasn't so different from their school in Park Slope. "Sixth graders are down there," said Mrs. Hitchens, bringing the twins to the edge of a hallway where the lockers were painted a deep, glossy brown. "Alex, you're 106. And Stella, you're next door. 107." Then she handed them slips of paper with numbers written on them. "Don't lose these or forget your combination. The penalty is reshelving duty at the library after school." Stella hadn't told her that she wouldn't have minded spending time in the school library anyway.

Now Stella and Alex waved goodbye to Simon as he headed off toward the fifth grade bank of bright red lockers. Stella sighed with relief. She hadn't realized how much of her anxiety had been from being near him. She thought back to that afternoon in the cemetery out in the woods, when she'd almost fainted on Margaret's gravestone. Alex had spent the rest of that day trying to convince her that ghosts were *not* real, that getting upset was exactly what Simon had wanted, that the best thing to do was to pretend she wasn't scared of *anything* anymore. But she'd found it nearly impossible to fake that.

Stella could feel the gaze of other students as she came

upon her locker, but she wasn't ready to meet their glances just yet. She spun the combination and opened the door. The slim dark space stared back at her, and she suddenly wondered if any students had ever been shoved inside. She peered around Alex's open door to see if he was freaking out as badly as she was, but she found him already unloading his lunch onto the shelf at the top and hanging his jacket on the hook just underneath. A *Chin-up, kiddo,* from Dad that morning would have meant everything. Stella hugged her purple satin jacket across her torso. Maybe it would be best if she just kept it on today. In case she got cold.

Someone pounded on the other side of Stella's open locker door, and she nearly dropped to the ground.

Stumbling back, she found a boy standing there, his mouth wide with shock. "I am SO sorry," he said. "I didn't mean to scare you."

Alex had already lunged in front of Stella. She caught her breath and then, red-faced, nudged her brother aside. "Are you *sure* about that?" She heard the words come out of her mouth, almost a threat.

To her surprise, the boy laughed. "Pretty sure." He held out his hand. "I'm Gordon Weinberger. Are you Stella and Alex?"

"How'd you know?" asked Alex.

The boy shrugged. "Only new faces at school this year. I just figured."

"Figured right," said Stella, finding more courage.

"I snooped your names at the office. Sorry . . . It's just, I heard you're living at Wildwyck, and I . . ." He turned red. "I think that place is *so* cool. I've always wanted to check it out."

"Our parents are fixing it up," said Alex.

"Oh wow. Kids used to go out there and sneak around, but I never got the chance because I live with my gramma and she doesn't really let me do anything."

"Too bad," said Alex.

"Kids used to sneak around at Wildwyck?" Stella asked.

Gordon shook his head. "Not at Wildwyck. *In* Wildwyck."

"That's . . . disturbing." Stella tugged her jacket even tighter.

"Oh, well, there are *tons* of abandoned places up here in the mountains. Old resorts from the fifties and sixties. Mansions. There's even this psychiatric hospital not far from here that they say is super haunted. I saw some TV show about it a few years back. Creeped me right out. Hey! I've even heard — " Gordon stopped. He chewed at his lip, suddenly looking sheepish.

"Heard *what*?" Alex asked.

"I — I shouldn't say. It's rude."

Why stop now? Stella wanted to ask. "You've heard Wildwyck is haunted too," she suggested. She wasn't surprised when Gordon nodded. She shrugged. "Our stepbrother Simon keeps trying to convince us the same."

"Has he seen anything?"

"He says he has," Alex answered. "We're not sure we believe him."

Not sure? Stella had to stop herself from scoffing. They'd been actively trying to *disbelieve* him for the past few months. "He's probably faking," Stella corrected. "He likes to . . . push buttons."

"But people died there," said Gordon.

Alex perked up. "Really? Who?"

"It's just what they say." The twins were quiet for a moment. Someone slammed a locker across the hall, and Stella flinched. Gordon went on. "Anyway, maybe I could come over sometime. Tell you a little bit more about what I've heard. Or we could just hang out. Do you like Frisbee?"

Alex nodded. "Yeah. Totally."

Again, Stella had to breathe slowly. Alex had never tossed around a Frisbee in his life, not even when they used to go to the athletic fields at Prospect Park with their dad. He'd been more of a digging in the dirt and playing with ants kind of kid.

"Cool." Gordon stepped back, wearing a pleased smile. "Well . . . See you around. Good luck on your first day."

"Thanks," said Stella. "Nice to meet you." She realized quickly that this was true.

Gordon winked and then made his way through the growing crowd.

Stella turned to her brother. "*Frisbee?*"

Alex laughed. "I can learn!"

CHAPTER EIGHT
ALEX

ALEX WAS GLAD his schedule didn't match up exactly with his sister's. It was sometimes difficult to get people to understand that even though they were twins, they were actual, individual human beings. Having only lunch and gym together felt right.

Stella looked uncomfortable when they went into separate homerooms, but Alex was certain she could handle it. She was stronger than she gave herself credit for.

Alex's day went smoothly enough. His teachers were friendly. He was especially excited about shop class. Ms. Woo had told them that their main project would be to design and build a small model car out of wood, and at the end of the quarter the students would race to see whose ended up being the most aerodynamic. Alex had already imagined a prototype. Something short, low to the ground, sleek, and painted fire-engine red.

One strange thing about Frost Meadow Middle School was that aside from Gordon, none of the students seemed to be particularly interested in making friends. In fact, Alex had gone out of his way in each classroom to say hello to at least one kid — a suggestion from Dr. Solomon — and all he'd gotten had been a brief *Hi* or sometimes only a grunt. Alex worried that they'd already made up their minds about him and had spread the word IGNORE.

A small town conspiracy?

So it was a slight relief when he entered the cafeteria to find his sister waving for him to sit with her out on the patio. A compact stone wall bordered the edge of the concrete, beyond which a wide field stretched off to the woods.

Stella looked distraught. She'd never taken off her jacket from that morning. Her cheeks were red, her eyes glazed. Maybe she was overheated? But then she said, "People here aren't very friendly, are they?" And he knew exactly what she was talking about, and exactly how she felt.

"Gordon seemed pretty nice," he answered, reassuring. Stella nodded. "So, at least we've got him."

"I haven't seen Simon all day."

"A miracle?" Alex answered with a grin.

She nodded and took a bite of her turkey sandwich.

Right then, Gordon came up from somewhere behind them. "Howdy! How's day one going so far?"

Stella nearly choked from surprise.

"Okay," said Alex, patting her back. "How about you, Gordon?"

"Meh. The usual. Just another school year with the same bunch of bozos." Now Stella smiled for real. "Don't worry about *them*. They're always slow to warm up when something is new. People don't call it Frost Meadow for nothing." It was like Gordon was reading their minds.

"I'm surprised we're not in any classes together," Alex

mentioned. "It would be cool if you could introduce us to some of your friends."

Gordon seemed to shrink slightly. "Yeah, I'm in a private room most of the day." Alex wasn't sure what that meant, and he didn't think he should ask. "Hey, tell me which teachers you've got, and I'll tell you how much you can get away with."

This made Stella chuckle. It was nice to see some of her nervousness seeping away. She gave Gordon a rundown of all her classes. Gordon had a response for each of them. "Ms. Robinson is really hard, but if you can get on her good side, she's also really nice." And, "Mrs. Chenail is like everyone's grandmother. If you forget to do an assignment or you fumble a quiz, whip up some tears and she'll take pity on you." And then, "Mr. Apple is the worst . . . You just have to grin and bear him."

When it was Alex's turn, he'd barely gotten out the name of his math teacher, Mr. Levinthal, before Gordon stopped him. "Oh wow, you've got Mr. L?" Alex nodded, curious. "You know he used to be a teacher at Wildwyck back when it was still a school for *bad boys*."

Bad boys? What a funny way to put it.

"I . . . *didn't* know that. I wonder why he didn't mention it?"

"Maybe he doesn't know your family is the one who bought it."

"I thought the Wildwyck School shut down a long time ago," said Stella. "If he worked there, he must have been super young. Either that, or he's older than he looks."

"I think it's a little bit of both. I bet he's got some good stories. We should ask him!"

"I don't know about that," said Alex. If most of the students had spent the morning observing the twins as if they were dissection specimens, who was to say the idea hadn't been caught by the teachers as well? "I'd like to survive a few more days here before . . . getting personal."

"That's fine," Gordon said, sounding disappointed. "Oh, I heard your stepbrother is having fun over in the fifth grade wing."

"Having *fun*?" Stella echoed.

"Yeah, I mean, apparently he's been sharing all these ghost stories and his classmates are loving it."

Alex felt a burning in his gut. Everyone had been looking at Alex and Stella like they were freaks, if they looked at them at all, and Simon was off using the family ghosts to make new friends. "It won't last."

After gym class, the twins ran into Simon outside the music room. He looked genuinely happy to see them. Alex tried to do the same, giving him big eyes and a wide fake smile. "I love it here!" Simon said.

"That's great, Simon," Stella answered. Alex was impressed. She'd managed to sound genuine.

"I met a bunch of kids and they all want to hang out. I'm as popular as Zachary."

"Zachary *is* pretty popular," Alex said.

When Simon squinted at him, Alex realized it might have come off as condescending. A change came over Simon. In an extra-loud voice, he said, as if for the whole hallway to hear, "Oh, I don't think Mrs. Hitchens is cranky at all. She's been nothing but *super sweet*. Why would you even say that, Alex?" Then he glanced over Alex's shoulder and waved. "Hi, Mrs. Hitchens!"

Alex spun to find the principal strolling up behind him. His skin prickled. Obviously, she'd heard Simon. Alex wanted to explain quickly that he hadn't called her cranky. That Simon was lying again, to get him in trouble. "Hello, Principal Hitchens," he said with a wave, trying to sound confident.

"And how are our newest students?"

"Really great!" Stella answered, overenthusiastically. "My classes are lots of fun, and my teachers are super inspiring." This gave Alex the chance to glare ice shards at Simon. Simon smiled back, infuriatingly. Mom and Charlie would hear about this later.

"That's wonderful." Mrs. Hitchens turned to the boys. "And you?"

"I've made lots of friends," said Simon. "So that's good."

Alex felt his brain shutting down. "I . . . I liked the patio."

"The patio?"

"At lunch," he went on, fighting a bout of tongue-tying. "Where me and Stella ate."

Mrs. Hitchens nodded, smiling politely. "A nice spot to sit and think." She clapped her hands and continued down the hall. "Let me know if I can help in any way." Her voice was almost singsong now, as if to prove to Alex that she was not, in fact, *cranky*.

When she was out of earshot, Alex leaned close to Simon and whispered, "What is *wrong* with you?"

"It was a joke!" Simon laughed. "Zachary would have laughed."

"I'm not Zachary!"

"That was the *principal*, Simon." Stella shook her head. "And this is the first day of school."

Simon's grin dropped away. "I know who that was. And I know what day it is. Don't talk to me like I'm a baby."

"Don't try and get me in trouble!" Alex spat.

"Look, I'm sorry. I wasn't thinking. It was a dumb thing to do," Simon said, bouncing slightly as he walked off. "So, I'll see you guys on the bus after the last bell. Unless you go and get yourself a detention, Alex. Be careful!"

Alex fumed as a couple fifth graders ran up to Simon, looking excited to chat. It took all his strength to not rush after him and . . . like, tie his shoelaces together.

Stella groaned. "Mom and Charlie are gonna love this."

"Why does he hate us so much?" Alex wondered aloud. "What did we do wrong?"

Stella murmured an answer that sounded like: "It's a mystery." Or maybe: "*He's* a mystery."

Both were true.

On the bus, Alex was happy when the seats around him and Stella filled up before Simon climbed aboard. Simon looked smugly toward the twins, then plopped himself next to a kid who immediately started up a conversation with him. Probably one of his fifth grade fans. Stella doodled another unicorn in her sketch pad. Alex reached into the front pocket of his book bag and removed the phone, which he'd kept switched off all day, as was the rule. He waited for it to boot up, excited to jot down an idea for a title. The back of a DVD box in the library had struck him as hilarious: rated PG for "Intense Zombie Action." *Intense Zombie Action* would make a perfect name for a rock band or maybe even a comic book! He chuckled as he pulled up the Notes app, but when he scrolled down, he nearly threw the phone to the floor.

"What's wrong?" Stella asked.

Alex trembled with anger. He turned the screen so his sister could see. His list was there, as usual. But several items were added to the bottom. Items that he definitely hadn't added himself. Stella read them tentatively, keeping her voice low. *"Alex Plays with Baby Toys."* Her expression growing more hurt with each line. *"A Horse Girl with a Horsey Face: The Stella Hill Story?"* She paused before reading the final one. *"What to Do When Daddy . . . Dies?"* She glared at him, shocked. Her eyes glistened. "Why would you write these things?" she said quickly, viciously. "Not funny, Alex. It's *sick*."

"You think *I* wrote them?"

"Who did?"

Alex stared forward, his glare piercing the occupant of the seat several rows ahead. Simon was laughing with his new friend, looking like he was trying very hard to not glance back.

CHAPTER NINE
STELLA

STELLA KNEW IT was a bad idea, but Alex was insistent.

Before the bus reached their driveway, Alex had asked Stella to keep Simon's shenanigans of the day to themselves. He'd even asked her to promise not to confront Simon about what he'd put into Alex's Notes. "We could mention it to Zachary," she'd suggested. "See what he says." But Alex didn't want to involve Simon's big brother.

Alex wanted revenge. And he wanted it to be a secret.

Simon had a wish to live in a haunted house? Alex and Stella would grant it.

Hiding in the den at the back of the house, he told her what to do. "You remember the song Simon was humming that day in the graveyard?"

Stella nodded. "I wish I could forget it."

Alex held up his phone, the voice recorder open. "Hum it for me." He hit record.

Stella had a moment of doubt. Her brother had refused to tell her the whole plan. He'd said that the less she knew, the better, so her reaction would be more *real*. But then she remembered what Simon had written in the Notes app. *A Horse Girl with a Horsey Face . . .* So she put her doubts aside and hummed into the mic.

Alex fiddled with the app and made Stella's voice loop. It played over and over. "Perfect," Alex whispered.

After sunset, when Charlie and Mom went out for a meeting in town, Alex invited Stella to watch television in the living room with him. The twins knew that Simon would insist on joining them. When he plopped down into the lounge chair at the end of the sofa, Alex even played it up by asking Simon what he felt like watching. Stella imagined an executioner taking a last meal request.

Simon shrugged. "*Steven Universe?*"

"Good choice," said Stella, flipping through the options. In the back of her mind she couldn't stop thinking, *Horsey Face.*

Halfway through the episode, Alex grabbed the remote and lowered the volume. "Do you hear that?"

"Hear what?" Stella asked, as she'd rehearsed.

Simon sat up, looking concerned. He tilted his head as if to listen.

"It sounds like . . . singing," said Alex.

Stella stood. "Isn't that . . ." She looked to Simon. "It's the song you were humming a couple weeks ago."

Simon strained harder. "I don't hear anything."

"Where's it coming from?" Alex asked.

Stella stepped into the hall. "Did you leave your stereo on upstairs?" she asked Alex. Wide-eyed, he shook his head. As Alex followed Stella, Simon scrambled to join them.

"Whoa." Simon's eyes bugged out. "I hear it now!"

Stella found herself feeling giddy, pressing her lips together to keep herself from smiling. She was getting into the act now, as if it were a game. And it *was* a game. At least, that's what Simon always called it. "It's coming from over here."

They reached the foyer. Alex had told her to stop there. To wait. To let Simon figure out the rest on his own. Clearly, the humming was coming from behind the door to the basement.

She watched as Simon approached, his ears pricked up. He turned and held a finger to his lips. Stella imagined abandoned kittens to keep herself from giggling. Miraculously, Alex stood stone-faced beside her.

The recorded voice warbled from behind the wood. *Mmm-mmm. Mmm-mmm-mmm-mmmmm.* Simon reached for the knob. The hinges squealed as he pulled the door open, showing shadows beyond that were darker than only an hour earlier.

Too dark. *Blinding* dark. The kind of dark that gives nightmares.

This wasn't right. Stella reached out to pull Simon back, but he stepped quickly through the doorway.

"Hello?" he called out, his voice echoing down into the passage.

Was something moving around in there? Something Stella could barely make out?

Alex bolted forward and slammed the door shut. The sound of Simon's shriek made Stella want to scream too. Alex grabbed a nearby chair and shoved it underneath the knob. His expression was almost as scary as what she thought she'd heard coming up from the darkness toward Simon. The door rattled and the chair quaked as Simon pounded and yelled. "Help! Let me out!" Alex burst out laughing. Stella went for the chair, but Alex blocked her and shook his head.

She wrapped her arms across her rib cage and thought of the terror she'd felt earlier that day, in the unfamiliar sixth grade hallway, unable to bring herself to take off her jacket, of the glazed stares of her new classmates who refused to say hello. She thought of Simon, surrounded by friends, all wanting to hear his stories, how he seemed as happy as a kid at the top of a playground slide. She thought of what he'd said in front of Mrs. Hitchens: *I don't think Mrs. Hitchens is cranky at all. Why would you even say that, Alex?*

And the Horse Girl comment.

The Horse *Face* comment.

She steeled herself.

"H-Help me!" Simon yelled, sobbing. Was he really that scared? Or was he faking, playing along? "P-Please!" It sounded real. She could practically hear snot rattling at the back of his throat. Simon deserved this. And yet —

A sound echoed from the kitchen. A scrape and a squeal. Like furniture dragged harshly across tile. It jolted Stella and Alex away from the basement door. There came a boom. Something large had tumbled over — shaking the kitchen floor, rattling the walls. Stella held back a cry. She glanced at her brother, whose brow was furrowed with worry. Did that mean this *wasn't* part of his plan?

The house shuddered again. From the kitchen came more banging sounds — *bam, bam, bam*. Stella peered through the doorway. All the cupboard doors had been opened. The kitchen table was lying upside down in the center of the floor. The chairs surrounding the table had been shoved back against the walls.

Stella reached for her brother's hand. "Alex," she whispered, "stop this."

He was staring into the kitchen too. Seeing the damage. "This isn't me," he answered flatly.

His words hit her like a shower of ice. It was a lie. Of course he was *doing something*. They both were. Her own humming continued to sound from behind the closed basement door, intermingled now with Simon's crying.

She moved toward the chair blocking her stepbrother's way out. She was about to yank it aside when another sound interrupted her, freezing her feet to the floor. A sound that came from behind the door where Simon was trapped.

A noise like an animal crying out for its first meal, like a stolen child who knows they'll never be rescued, like a beast crunching bones, a tree toppling in a storm, waves crashing on jagged rocks, a siren blaring loud enough to wake the world. All these things, mixed-up, made more terrible.

Stella nearly fell to the floor.

The sound went on and on, dampening the recording of the humming and drowning out Simon's voice. Before she could think to move again, Alex had grabbed at her wrist and pulled her to the front door. Together, they dashed out into the night.

As soon as they set foot outdoors, the clamor inside the house halted. Stella could still hear it ringing in her skull, and for several seconds, she worried its echo would be endless.

Then softly, as if from far away, she heard: "Help! Let me out!"

"Simon!" She tried the front door, but the latch wouldn't budge.

"It's dark! I can't see!" Simon's voice was fainter now.

Stella looked to Alex. "What did you do?" He grappled with the front door himself. "Was *all of this* part of your plan?"

"Of course not!"

"Then what made that noise? Who messed up the kitchen?"

Alex pounded on the door, then kicked it. Nothing worked. They were stuck outside. "I don't know," he spat. "Maybe . . . Maybe it was Simon. Maybe he knew what we were up to. Maybe he set *us* up."

"Help!" Simon cried again. Stella thought about how loudly he must be screaming if they could hear him from outside.

"But he's just a kid," said Stella. "Those noises were . . . They were . . ."

Alex stepped away from the house. He glanced at the two darkened wings and then stared at the one in the center, which was lit up like a shield against the shadows. "You think *kids* can't do bad things?" he asked. "Look where we live. They used to send them here."

A chill seeped through Stella's shirt. The building appeared to be staring back at them, its blackened windows hiding secrets. "What do we do?" Stella whispered.

An answer came as a pair of headlights swept across the courtyard.

CHAPTER TEN
ZACHARY

September 2

Earlier tonight, Dad and Bev told us that they were headed out to a town meeting, which was a LIE. I know this because I saw a weird bill on the dining room table a couple days ago, and when I looked up the name at the top of the page, it turned out to be a marriage counselor. I mean, good for them if the therapist is helping. That's what they do, right? Help?

But the fact that they're lying about it to us might mean it's not.

I bet Simon would be happy to hear about Dad and Bev's troubles. Maybe he'll finally get to go back and live with Mom. Or maybe he won't. Maybe we all just stay here, trapped in this house, miserable together.

Talking about being miserable together, get this:

The twins and Simon are in SO MUCH TROUBLE. It's almost funny how much trouble they're in. And strange too, because I was up in the attic doing my homework with my headphones on and didn't hear a single sound of them literally destroying the house!

An hour or so after Dad and Bev said goodbye, I was just starting my algebra when I hear, or maybe it wasn't so much HEAR, but I FELT this banging. My desk was rattling, and when I took off my headphones, it sounded like there was someone pounding frantically on the front door.

I race down the stairs to find Simon barricaded inside the basement stairwell. He's screaming and yelling as if something was clawing at him. So I pull away the chair and he bursts out and lands on his face.

Just then Dad comes in through the front door with Bev and the twins and they're all shouting at each other. Supposedly, Stella and Alex had managed to lock themselves out of the house. Dad looks mad because the front door wasn't even bolted, but the twins keep yelling that it _had_ been. And that it's Simon's fault.

That's when they see Simon lying on the floor, whimpering. Bev sits him up and asks what happened. He tells them about the basement door. And I show them the chair that was keeping it propped shut. Simon looks surprised and hurt and then scowls at Alex and Stella. Then Dad asks, What's that noise?

I realize someone's singing, or humming. Dad goes over to the stairwell, and Alex shouts, WAIT, but of course Dad doesn't wait. He's just inside the basement doorway, listening. He reaches atop the frame and plucks away a phone that was taped to the wall. And since Alex was the one who'd screamed WAIT, we all have a very good idea who it belongs to.

Turns out, the twins had been playing a trick on Simon to get him back for... who knows what at this point? But things had gone _awry_.

Bev screamed when she saw the state of the kitchen. Tables and chairs overturned. All the cabinet doors opened. Dad demanded to know what they'd been doing.

Stella blamed Simon again...who, LEST WE FORGET, had been trapped in the stairwell!

Liar, I say. I couldn't help it. The word just popped out of my mouth. Stella stared at me in disbelief. I'd never spoken up against the twins before, but then I'd never seen them try and hurt my brother before. Alone in the dark, confused, and terrified. I know Simon has been playing tricks on them. But what if he'd slipped and fallen down the stairs? Broken his neck?

Okay, okay, says Dad. I think we've all had enough excitement for one night. Everyone upstairs. We'll deal with this in the morning. He looks to Bev, who nods.

How was the town meeting? I ask.

They glance at each other, worried, as if I'd touched on something sensitive, which I knew I had. Then Bev looks me right in the eye and says, It was good. We were able to ask some questions to the Historical Society. So hopefully, we'll be able to make some progress this weekend.

I had to keep from laughing. Another lie. But one that worked. Dad and Bev had been talking for a while about how the Historical Society's restrictions keep them from getting work done. And it made me think:

The most effective lies are the ones that have a seed of truth inside them.

Anyway, Simon is snoring now. And my bed is calling to me.
Your friend,
Zachary Kidd

CHAPTER ELEVEN
ALEX

ON SATURDAY MORNING, the twins went up to the barn.

They told Mom and Charlie that they were going to organize the mess in there, since they were now grounded, but really, they were desperate to get out of the house. Alex wanted to explore. And Stella still dreamed of reviving the horse stable, just like in the old days of the estate.

Now they were knee-deep in disaster. Rusted tools were scattered across the floor. Boxes and crates had been crammed with newspaper-wrapped whatevers. Furniture, so water damaged that the wood had become brittle, lay about, some of it in pieces.

"Keep or throw out?" Stella asked, holding up the oxidized blade of a giant scythe, its wooden handle missing.

"Keep, obviously," Alex answered after a glance. "And careful with that. Could take off your hand." Inside this new crate were a bunch of tiny glass bottles, crusted with dirt. Some even had cork stoppers and liquid inside. Alex held one up to the light. The contents looked like a potion. Maybe he could use it later on Simon to turn him into a better sibling. With his luck, however, the kid would probably end up in a coma.

In the few days since "the incident," the twins had talked a lot about what had gone down in the kitchen, with the furniture and cabinets and the growling sound. Alex was convinced Simon knew perfectly well what the twins had planned, and he'd arranged his own version of a haunting to get them back. He could've asked Zachary for advice, since Zachary was as into all this ghostly and spooky stuff as Simon. Stella still wasn't sure. She'd even dared to suggest that Alex had set *all* of it up, since he'd kept her in the dark about most of it. She apologized right after, but Alex was still hurt she thought he would do something so cruel.

"Keep or throw out?" Stella asked again. This time, it was a rotted straw hat, infected with mildew and a hole punched through its center. A moment later, Stella busted out laughing and then tossed it into the garbage pile.

A train horn sounded in the distance, rolling toward them from across the hills. It reminded Alex of the church bells that used to ring throughout Park Slope every Sunday morning — evidence of life happening elsewhere. He wondered what he and Stella might be doing right now if they were still in the city. Karate class with Dad in Prospect Park? An herbal hunt around the Brooklyn Botanic Garden, one of Dad's favorite spots in all of New York City? Or maybe an early brunch on the penthouse deck of their father's friends' place, who lived across from the Brooklyn Museum. You could see the whole city from up there. Standing next to Dad, who pointed out the details of that view, had once been the whole world.

Dr. Solomon had told Alex many times that these memories were a connection to his father, but he was sure they only made him miss Dad even more. And that only made him mad. Made him wish he had something else to focus on, like Stella with her drawings and her horses. Mom had even been looking into riding lessons for her. But what was up in these mountains for *him*?

Footsteps crunched through the grass outside the barn, and Alex glanced nervously at Stella. It wasn't a ghost he was worried about. It was their stepbrother.

To his relief, Charlie appeared in the wide doorway of the barn. To his surprise, however, there was a boy standing beside him.

Gordon Weinberger.

"You have a visitor," said Charlie. His tone and the sour look on his face told them he wasn't happy about it.

Gordon gave a sheepish wave.

"Gordon," Stella said, putting down a large ceramic planter and stepping over the rest of the debris. "What are you doing here?"

"I walked up from the village," he answered, looking to Charlie. "I didn't realize you were *grounded*." There was a brief glint of amusement in his eyes. "I don't have your phone number. Otherwise, I would have called."

Charlie sniffed. "I'll write it down before you go."

Stella looked crestfallen. "Oh, Charlie, you're not going to send Gordon all the way back into Frost Meadow, are you? It's such a long walk!"

"I could drive him," Charlie said, a slight drawl in his voice. Alex could tell he was teasing. "However . . . I'm happy to let Gordon be your chump, if that's what he wants." Gordon chuckled and stepped into the barn. "Be good," said Charlie, turning back toward the house. Sometimes their stepdad could be pretty cool. He called over his shoulder, "Your mom and I are working in the south wing today if you need us."

"And where's Simon?" Stella asked.

Smart, thought Alex. The kid could be spying on them right now.

"Should be up in his room, unpacking the rest of his boxes. You know, the ones we were supposed to clear out *last week*?" He shook his head and continued on.

"I haven't met him yet," said Gordon.

"That's just as well," said Stella. "He can be . . ." She sighed. "Very little brotherish."

"I wouldn't know," said Gordon. "I've only ever had my grandmother." He looked around. "Wow, this stuff is awesome." He examined the piles that Stella had made.

"More like *apocalyptic*," said Alex.

"I like your apocalypse. I'll bet you find treasure." Gordon wandered deeper into the barn, disappearing behind some of the bigger pieces of stacked furniture. "I can't believe *this* is your punishment," he called out. "Lucky you weren't locked in the attic, or worse!"

"Careful back there," said Alex. "We haven't checked if it's stable."

"Stable," Stella called out, with a weird grin. When Gordon didn't answer, she shrugged awkwardly. "Get it? There are horse stalls. One day, I'm going to buy a couple painteds. My mom's looking to sign me up for riding lessons."

"That's fun," came Gordon's voice. "So, what got you all grounded?"

Alex groaned. "We had a fight with Simon," he answered.

"Must have been a pretty big fight."

Alex found Gordon crouched in front of an antique dresser five drawers tall, high enough that its top came to just below Alex's nose.

"Check this out," Gordon whispered. The bottom drawer was open. Alex wasn't sure if Gordon had opened it or if he'd found it that way. Gordon removed a metal box. "See? There might be treasure here after all."

CHAPTER TWELVE
SIMON

WHILE THE TWINS were out in the barn, Charlie had made Simon promise to leave them alone and unpack the boxes that he hadn't gotten around to yet. This made Simon steam. Why should Alex and Stella get to go out and practically *play*, while he was left in his attic bedroom? As soon as he heard his dad and Bev turn on their table saw in one of the renovation wings, he crept downstairs and slipped out the back door.

He ran from the house. To get far from view, he hopped over the stone wall that came down from the woods, then he crouched down.

After what the twins had done to him, locking him in the basement stairwell, he planned on breaking all sorts of rules. Fair was fair. Sure, he'd probably deserved some sort of payback for the trick he'd played on Alex in front of the principal, but getting locked in the dark staircase like that? The recording? The humming? And whatever they'd done to the kitchen? And they said that *he* took things too far. Although, the planning they must have done to pull it off was kind of impressive.

Maybe Stella and Alex were as wild as Simon imagined himself to be. If that were true, could they maybe become wilder together?

The grass on the other side of the wall was nearly up to

Simon's waist. Later, he'd have to check himself all over for ticks, but for now, he wanted to get close to the barn without anyone noticing. Walking low through the grass, he tried to think of a way to surprise the twins, but then the ground was gone beneath him. Simon reached out to catch himself, but his fingers slipped through long strands of grass. He didn't even have time to cry out.

His knees hit the ground. He rolled onto his side. His shoulder smashed into damp sod, and he thought he heard something crack, but after he'd caught his breath and managed to sit up, he realized that nothing was broken. Looking skyward, he could see a circle of blue, obscured by evil-looking weeds that had caved in toward him.

A deep hole had been hidden by the overgrown vegetation. He'd fallen in. He remembered his dad saying that there were old wells and abandoned cisterns around the property and to only stay in areas where the grass was trim until he'd had a chance to clearly mark them.

Simon sighed and then stood. Thankfully, the pit wasn't *that* deep. No more than six feet. This wouldn't be one of those kids-trapped-down-a-well situations you'd hear about on the news. Still, he couldn't help feeling like a dum-dum.

The space was wide enough for him to stretch out his arms. He tried to leverage his way up by pressing his feet and his spine back against the stone sides of the hole, but he wasn't tall enough to make it work. He jumped and tried to grab for the ledge, but it was too far. Was the only option to call for help? If the twins came to his rescue, would they make him beg?

He did *not* want to beg.

A crunching sound echoed from above — footsteps through the grass. "Hey!" Simon yelled. "Watch where you step!" It wasn't exactly a cry for help, which made him feel proud, and whoever it was could pull him up into daylight. (It was a little late to worry about being caught red-handed.) The footsteps seemed to stop just at the edge of the hole.

Looking up, Simon barely made out the silhouette of someone peering down at him. "I fell," he said. "Can you help me?"

But the silhouette only continued to stare.

Simon felt his face get hot. "Alex? Stella?"

No answer.

He crouched and pressed his spine against the embankment, not taking his eyes off the dark shape peering silently down at him. His heart thumped. His scalp tingled. A coldness seeped from the ground, and he wished he'd worn a jacket.

After what felt like a long while, with the figure showing no sign of movement, Simon began to wonder if maybe it was just a stump or stone he hadn't noticed earlier. If maybe he'd misheard wind through the grass as footsteps.

"Stupid," he whispered.

There was a chuckle. When Simon flicked his gaze upward, the silhouette dipped away. Goose bumps coated his skin. His voice dried up. Someone *had* been watching — sitting there staring, saying nothing, not offering help.

Then laughing.

Instantly, Simon's fear was replaced by anger. "Alex! I'm telling my dad about this! You're SOOO getting grounded . . . *More* grounded!"

Muffled chuckling sounded beyond the lip of the hole as if whoever had been watching him was now covering their mouth, as if they would wait for him to try and crawl out on his own, and then they'd point and laugh and guffaw and then run and tell everyone what a moron Simon Kidd truly was.

"Jerk!" Simon yelled.

The laughing continued.

But . . .

It didn't sound like either of the twins. It was lower. Raspier. Like someone with a sore throat. Hearing it only made Simon angrier. He'd climb up, chase down whoever this was, and throw dirt in their face.

"Stop laughing!"

But it went on, as if the person wasn't amused anymore, but was trying to see if they could make Simon pop.

"STOP!"

Then it did stop. But it was replaced with a harsh growl.

Simon clamped his mouth shut. His eyes went supernova. He clenched his fists. This was the sound he'd heard the other night when the twins had locked him in the stairwell. It was the sound he'd imagined he'd heard behind that old door in the basement a couple weeks ago. This wasn't the twins. It wasn't a prank.

It was the ghost.

Staring up into the sunburst circle of grass-shaded sky, Simon wasn't sure he wanted to leave the pit anymore. It felt safer down in the dark.

But only until something near his feet shifted and slithered toward him.

CHAPTER THIRTEEN
SIMON

SIMON YELPED AND jumped away.

Was it a mouse? A snake?

A skeletal hand?

The thing moved again. A rustling echoed. He leapt back, his fingers scraping at the side of the pit. Simon pulled against a piece of the wall. A large stone tilted forward. He shifted backward. It landed with a soft thud between his sneakers. He stepped on it to get away from whatever was crawling around.

He found another jutting stone and yanked it loose. It plopped to the ground. He did this again and again until he had a pile. Though it was wobbly, he climbed up and heaved himself toward the ledge, grasping at the long grass. As he dangled, chest against the stones, breath shallow, heart revving, he imagined who might be waiting for him up there. The little ghost girl from the graveyard? (Hadn't he made her up? He couldn't remember anymore.) Or was it something else? A thing that could growl. A thing with teeth that bite. He strained, kicking at the wall, gained stability, then reached farther for a better grip. Gradually, he worked his way up. Once out of the hole, he kept himself low. Pivoting slowly, he took in the entire field. He didn't see anyone, but then they might rise up suddenly beside him and shove him back down into the pit. He'd hit his head on the loose rocks and knock himself out.

He'd die out here, if they let him.

A tightness in his chest prompted him to jump to his feet. "Leave me alone!" He said it so loudly, his throat hurt.

For a moment, he wasn't even sure who he was yelling at. The twins? His father? Bev?

Zachary?

No one answered. Nothing moved in the grass, at least not anywhere nearby.

Could it all have been in his head? The silhouette, the laughing, the growl? Maybe he'd bumped his skull on his way down. Simon took a deep, slow breath. The grass wavered in the soft breeze. He brushed chills from his arms.

Laughter skipped down the hillside, and Simon stiffened. He glanced toward the barn, where Alex and Stella were apparently "working." So then, the person he'd heard, the growling thing, it hadn't been the twins.

Still . . . Did he really want to be around them now? To have them stare at him with hatred? It would be better than standing out here, alone. Wouldn't it? Simon turned to the dark patch from which he'd climbed. The hole was nearly invisible. He knelt and grappled with the tall grass. Working up a sweat, he pulled out every clump, every root of the pit's disguise, tossing the grass inside so that when he was finished, it looked like an empty eye socket staring blindly at the sun. "There," he whispered. "You won't get me again."

He found a stick lying nearby, a pale branch that must have blown down during some summer storm. He picked it up. Making his way back toward the wall, he tapped at the ground before each step. Every now and again, he raised the stick like a staff, like a character in that video game Zachary was always playing — a paladin? — and then spun, to scare anyone who might be following at his heels. At the wall, he climbed onto the well-worn trail.

The voices of the twins came down the hill again, but then Simon noticed a third. A lower voice. A raspier voice. One that reminded him of the chuckling he'd heard when he'd been down in the pit, which, strangely, now seemed like a distant memory.

Simon raced up the path. He snuck around the edge of the wide door. It was the first time he'd gotten a good whiff of the staleness in the barn. Mildew. Mold.

Where were the twins hiding?

The barn was filled with junk. He stared through the shadows toward the rear of the building. The stacks were higher back there. He stepped inside, gripping the paladin staff tightly.

From somewhere back down the hill, an animal barked. Whined. The sound made Simon nervous. Then he heard whispering deeper in the barn. "Alex? Stella?" he called out.

To Simon's surprise, a boy he'd never seen before stepped out from behind a wooden wardrobe. The boy was tall, or at least taller than Simon. His hair was longish and sandy-colored. The whites of his eyes stood out around deep brown irises. And when he smiled, his teeth seemed almost blindingly bright. He wore an old pair of faded jeans and a blue ringer T-shirt that looked like it had come from a thrift shop. He eased through the maze of junk, holding his hand out to Simon, as if in introduction. In his other hand was a metal box.

Simon raised his staff before himself, unsure why he suddenly felt unsafe. He was about to run back to the house when —

"Hello there," the boy said, ignoring Simon's fearful stance. "You must be Simon. I'm Gordon. Nice to meet you finally, face-to-face."

CHAPTER FOURTEEN
STELLA

STELLA WATCHED GORDON approach her stepbrother near the barn's entrance. At first she didn't notice Simon's disheveled state. But as her vision grew accustomed to the daylight outside, she could see that something was wrong. His clothes were stained with mud and grass. His T-shirt was ripped near the collar. Blood was trickling down his legs from gashes on both knees. He had a small cut on his cheek. And his eyes were swollen.

She nudged Alex. When he saw Simon, he raised an eyebrow, in *not-quite* concern.

"How do you know my name?" Simon asked, a quavering in his voice.

"Your brother and sister told me." He gave Stella and Alex a happy wave.

Simon squinted. "They're my *step*brother and my *step*sister."

Stella was surprised. Simon usually waited at least a couple minutes before bringing on THE RUDE.

"I hear that you and me might have a lot in common," Gordon replied, unintimidated.

"Oh yeah?"

"You like to tell ghost stories about this place . . . I like to hear them."

Simon brightened. "Really?"

Before the two could become fast friends, Stella stepped forward. "Simon, what the heck happened to you?"

He froze, considering how to answer. He looked over his shoulder, toward the field and the stone wall that crossed it. "I fell."

Alex laughed. "You *fell*? It looks like you walked through a firefight."

Simon tilted his head. "And that's funny?"

Alex scoffed. "I'm just *saying* . . ."

Simon looked to Gordon. "What's in the box?"

"Oh!" Gordon held it out before himself. "We haven't opened it yet."

He knelt, then waved for the others to do the same. Simon tried but flinched when his knees touched the ground, so he sat cross-legged instead. Stella and Alex crouched as Gordon raised the lid and tilted the box toward them. Inside, a few items shifted.

One by one, he lifted them out. The first was a silver chain. Stella felt almost mesmerized by the crescent moon pendant that swung from the bottom. As she looked closer, she noticed a tiny fairy perched as if on a swing, its wings spread wide. A minuscule crown glinted atop its head. Jewel flecks? Or maybe they were glass. Next, Gordon removed a small, leather-bound book, the brown cover worn at the edges and cracked along the spine. When he flipped through the pages, most appeared crinkled and stiff, damaged by water. Black ink blurred into a washed-out purple. Whatever had been written there had mostly bled away.

Gordon plucked one last item from the bottom of the box. He held it up, turning it slowly, so each of them could see. It was a faded Polaroid photograph. A picture of a girl with long, dark curls, pale skin, and blue eyes, peering over her shoulder at the photographer. The image was blurred, as if she'd been caught in motion. She looked like she was about to smile or laugh, and something in her gaze gave a clue to her kindness.

Stella felt an immediate connection. *Margaret*, she thought, remembering the cemetery over the hill.

Alex shifted uncomfortably beside her, and Simon's eyes sparked. Gordon's thumb was partially covering some writing at the bottom of the picture. "Can I see?" Stella asked. He handed it over. Written in faded ballpoint pen: *P. ~ 1975.* "*P*?" she asked. "Who is *P*?"

"Weird. I thought maybe this stuff belonged to Margaret Wildwyck," Alex suggested.

"How do you know about her?" Gordon asked, quizzically.

Stella sat up. "We found her grave a couple weeks ago — "

"*I* found the grave," Simon interrupted.

"*Right,*" said Stella evenly, not wanting to start something. "*Simon* found the grave."

"There's a whole mess of them out in the woods," Simon added. "A family plot." He held out his hand to Gordon. "Come see it!"

Gordon shook his head. "S'all right. I've already been back there."

"Do you know anything about her?" Alex asked. "Margaret, I mean. What can you tell us?"

"Not much. The stories I have are mostly about the Wildwyck school. Are you sure you want to hear them?"

All at once, Stella, Alex, and Simon chimed, "Yes!"

Gordon sat back on his heels, looking satisfied. He thought for a moment. "Well, you already know this was a school where people sent the *bad boys*."

"Bad boys?" Simon repeated. Stella thought it was funny how he almost sounded scared, like there might be places people sent kids like himself.

"Kids from the city, or even close by, who needed . . . special attention? My grandmother says the school was really good at getting students back on track. Some of the graduates were very successful. There are famous athletes from here. A couple actors and singers too. I can't remember names, but you'd definitely know them if you looked them up."

"That's pretty cool," said Alex. "Maybe one of them lived in *my* room."

"Or mine!" Simon chirped, not to be outdone.

"After a while, the school started having problems. Gramma says that the headmaster and his wife, Hart and Ada Wildwyck, were strange. They used to punish students by locking them in . . . *special* rooms. There were three in total. Each one had a name. The Cheaters' Room, for the boys caught cheating on their lessons. The Temper Room, for the boys who got in too many fights. And then there was the Liars' Room. Which . . . I mean . . . Sounds pretty obvious, right? They say that last one was the scariest, because it was pitch-black dark. You did *not* want to get caught lying at the Wildwyck School."

Liars' Room. The sound of it had sent shivers crawling underneath Stella's skin.

Gordon went on. "So, everyone in Frost Meadow knew about these punishment rooms, right? The weird thing was, in all the exploration the local kids did here when the school was abandoned, no one ever found any evidence of them."

"But there's that door in the basement," Simon whispered. "That's *got* to be where the Liars' Room is."

"Maybe," Stella answered, rubbing at her arms.

"You don't believe me?" Gordon looked surprised.

"I mean, it's not that I don't believe *you*." Stella glanced at Alex for support. "It's just . . . These are stories your grandmother told you? How do you know if she's right?"

Gordon's mouth lifted into a soft, sad smile. "There are people in Frost Meadow who cannot forget."

"Like Mr. Levinthal," said Alex. "My math teacher. You told me he used to work at the school, way back when he was just starting out."

Gordon perked up. "That's right."

"But what happened to Margaret?" Stella wanted to know. She couldn't explain it, but she felt a connection to the poor girl. "How did she . . . die?"

"The headmaster's daughter?" Gordon's face grew strangely somber. "I heard she got sick. Pneumonia, I think."

"But that's *boring*," said Simon.

Gordon flinched. Stella shook her head. But Alex leaned forward, fire in his eyes. "We'll all have to make sure that when *you* go, it's much more exciting."

Simon crossed his arms, unperturbed. "Please do," he answered.

After a moment, they all doubled over laughing.

Even Simon.

CHAPTER FIFTEEN
STELLA

LATER, STELLA SAT on her bed, staring at a blank page in her sketchbook. Ideas whirled through her imagination, but none of them seemed interesting enough to put down on paper. Looking up, she saw the metal box perched on top of her dresser. It made her think of music, of the tune Simon had hummed, the one Alex had asked her to put on the recording to scare Simon.

She could hear it somehow. But was it in her head? Was it somewhere far away, or right here in the bedroom playing ever so softly? She crawled across the mattress and listened. Something inside the box clicked, and she scooted back again. Gordon's stories from earlier in the day tingled her spine, and she felt suddenly frozen.

"Alex?" she called out toward the darkened hall.

A moment later, he appeared in her doorway.

"What's up?"

"The box." She nodded toward it. "It's creeping me out."

Alex wandered into the room and picked it up. He snorted, amused. "It's only a box, Stella."

"What if . . . Something at Wildwyck wanted us to find it and open it up?"

"That would be highly unlikely." Alex sat at the end of

her bed, placing the box between them. Stella couldn't take her eyes off it. What if it made another noise? What if it started to sing?

She shuddered. Suddenly, it was all too much. "I don't want to be here anymore. I don't want to live in a haunted place."

"We have to live here, Stella. This is what Mom and Charlie decided on."

"I don't care," she whispered. "I want . . . I want my old bedroom. I want . . . Dad . . . to come in at night and read me stories like he used to."

Alex sighed. "I mean, if you think about it, for us, that *old* apartment is the place that's really haunted. By truly scary things: memories."

"Dad was never scary. My *memories* of him aren't scary."

"Not the memories of him. The memories of *what happened* to him. Those are what give me nightmares. What wake me up at night wanting to . . ." Alex shuddered. Stella grabbed at his hand. "Maybe . . . Being here in Frost Meadow will help make that stop."

"Hasn't helped me so far." She sighed.

"What if . . . What if we came up with a plan?" he said. "Gordon threw a real big mud pie at us today with all that info. What if we try to figure out what *really* happened at Wildwyck? Learn its history? I think it might help make this place feel, like . . . normal? It could be like turning on all the lights at night. The more we know, the more we see. The less creeped out we are. Does that make sense?"

Stella nodded. She reached for the metal box. "Should we start with this?"

Alex sat up on his heels. "I mean, why not?"

Moments later, Stella had laid the contents of the box on the bedspread between them. There was the book, the necklace, and the Polaroid.

CHAPTER SIXTEEN
ALEX

HE COULD SEE by the look on her face that this would be a good idea. He'd always found that having a goal made life feel less uncertain, less scary, whether it was a finish line, a better running time, a completed model, a finished jigsaw, or obtaining the last official figurine in a Mystery Minis collection. Simon liked to play games with his older brother, Zachary. Heck, Simon would even play games with strangers if it would get him some attention. This box could be *their* game. This building — its mysteries — the twins would control it all.

As Stella flipped through the water- and ink-stained pages, Alex noticed some words that hadn't been blurred entirely. "Wait. Let me see that." Stella slid the book across the mattress. Alex pressed the pages to keep them open. *"New friend, J . . . A special connection . . ."* Alex flipped through them until he came to readable words. *"Mom and Dad won't let . . . Needs help . . . a's family is gone . . . We're meeting up again tonight. He says he has lots to tell me . . ."* He glanced at Stella. "It's a diary. Who do you think it belonged to?"

Stella touched the photo of the girl. "P?"

Alex nodded. Maybe this *would* keep her from imagining ghosts. "And J? And A? And who they're meeting up with?"

"Don't know," said Stella. "Can you make out any more?"

Alex peeled through every page. "Not really. There's got to be more here at Wildwyck. Clues to help us figure out what happened back then."

Stella smiled. "To turn on all the lights."

Alex chuckled. "Exactly. Let's see what we can find tomorrow."

Stella picked up the Polaroid and stared at it. She turned it over and ran her finger over the writing there. "1975," she whispered. With a glint in her eye, as if remembering something important, she looked up at him again. "That was the date on the grave out in the woods. Margaret Wildwyck. It was the year she died."

CHAPTER SEVENTEEN
ZACHARY

September 5

It's getting close to midnight, so I'll try to keep it short, but I have a lot to say.

Since the rest of the family is apparently grounded for the next week, I spent the day with Joshua and his friends. His sister, Teresa, drove some of us to this weird town, maybe an hour west, up in the mountains, called Hedston, where there was a huge abandoned building by a lake, way out in the woods.

When we got there, we found that the entire property had been blocked off with a chain-link fence, and there were KEEP OUT signs hanging all over the place. I asked them, Where are we? And Peggy said it was an old psychiatric hospital called Graylock.

The word sort of set off this strange fluttering in my chest, because I was sure that I'd heard it before. Wasn't it on one of those ghost-hunting television shows? I knew then that they planned to break in. It wasn't something I was really into, but I didn't want to look like a wuss. So when Joshua held open the gap in the fence and everyone crawled through, I followed.

We walked up an overgrown path. And Joshua was telling everyone about the three patients who had supposedly drowned in the water nearby, and I didn't want to listen, because even though I like scary stories, when they're real, it feels like too much.

Peggy hung back with me. I think she sensed what I was feeling. We're in a couple classes together and we've had some interesting conversations in the past few days. Like, about life and death. And the universe. She likes talking about the planets, and for some reason, I like listening.

It's not a crush or anything like that. It's more like... a special connection. Like, I could tell her some of the things I've only ever written down here in my journal.

The building is thick stone and covered in moss and just like...WET. Joshua finds an open window. And Peggy says, I think I want to stay out here. She turns to me and goes, Zachary should keep me company. And of course Doug and Myron and Leroy all start making kissing noises, but Teresa tells them to knock it off, which I appreciated, because of course that's not what it was about.

Peggy only wanted to stay outside because she knew I did too.

So there we waited... And waited... And waited. Until the others all came crawling back out. And we asked them how it was, and Myron said it was actually pretty boring. Most of the old hospital equipment had been cleared out, so there wasn't even anything spooky to look at.

Besides the actual building? I asked.

And Doug and Leroy laughed, admitting they did feel something weird inside. As if eyes were watching them. Following them. Arms outstretched, just at their heels, as if ready to *grab them and drag them into the shadows. Nurse Janet, they whispered.*

Riiiiiiight.

Joshua mentioned that the visit was a success because he managed to put up at least ten of his stickers, and he even tagged an actual door somewhere upstairs, with the number thirteen on it.

He said he felt vibes coming from inside.

Vibes? What the heck are <u>vibes</u>?

So I get home after dark and of course, my family is acting all weird. I find Simon upstairs in our room with bandages covering both of his knees. I ask him what he did to himself, and he tells me this story about falling into a hole, and how he saw someone watching him, someone who wouldn't help, and how he was certain it was Wildwyck's ghost. I nodded and tried to calm him down, even though I knew it was yet another lie, because that's what my little brother is.

A liar.

I decided to tell Bev and Dad, because obviously, now Simon's lies are <u>hurting</u> him.

When I went down to the bedroom on the first floor, I noticed their door was closed. They hadn't heard me coming and kept talking, sort of loudly. I held my ear against the door, and, well...I don't think their therapy is working very well.

Bev was going on and on about Simon and how she thought he was a bad influence on the twins. And then Dad chimes in and says that the twins aren't any better. And he goes on to say that if Bev can't love his kids the way she loves her own, then maybe this whole <u>family</u> thing just isn't going to work out. And Bev agreed! She demanded that Dad consider sending Simon back to Ohio. Which, to be honest, I don't think Simon would have a problem with. But that's not the point.

The point is the anger I felt coming from inside that room. Maybe that's what Joshua meant by <u>vibes</u>.

Anyway, if this goes on too much longer, I think I might just…lose my marbles. Good thing Graylock isn't open for business anymore, otherwise Bev might consider sending <u>me</u> there.

I wish it wasn't so late. I really want to talk to Peggy again. She always manages to calm me down.

Your friend,

Zachary Kidd

CHAPTER EIGHTEEN
ALEX

ON SUNDAY, ALEX woke up clearheaded for the first time in days. He felt good about the agreement he and Stella had made the night before, to research the history of Wildwyck and find answers to its strange questions.

They managed to avoid Simon through breakfast, and afterward, when they ran into their parents in the foyer, Charlie and Mom were on their way to the south wing for another round of renovations.

"Remember, you're grounded," Mom said just before she closed the front door. "Please just . . . *Be good.*"

"We will be," said Alex.

"Of course, Mom," Stella answered.

Mom gave a pleading look before heading off with Charlie.

Stella grabbed at Alex's wrist. "Where do we start?" He glanced at the basement door under the landing, the one they'd shut their stepbrother inside that past Wednesday. Stella shook her head.

"We should at least go check out the old door Simon said was down there. Maybe we can get it open."

"I feel weird sneaking around right after what Mom just said," Stella whispered.

"Mom and Charlie have different priorities at the moment," Alex concluded.

They approached the stairwell together. The landing inside stretched forward several feet before plunging into gloom. Alex strained to see the bottom.

"Hold on," said Stella. She rushed into the kitchen, returned with a flashlight, and cast a pale beam into the basement hallway below.

Though he'd been planning all this to help his sister fight her fear, Alex suddenly found himself getting shaky.

At the bottom, the plaster walls made the hall feel like a tomb. Since Stella was holding the flashlight, she squeezed past him so they'd have a better view. She reached up and grabbed at the string. The bulb wasn't bright, but it was stronger than the flashlight. A few cords hung from the electric socket and ran up the passage and around the corner. The wires were tangled. There were damp spots on the dirt floor. An accident waiting and all that jazz. Alex understood why Charlie hadn't wanted them to come down here. But how could they go back now?

Ahead, the hallway turned sharply where it met the school's old stone foundation. Stella ran her finger along the ancient mortar and it crumbled at her touch. "Whoa. Mom and Charlie have so much work cut out for them."

Around the bend, the light from the hall barely spilled halfway across a small room. Still, Alex could make out some of Charlie's tools propped against the walls. There was a shovel. A rake. A wheelbarrow. A wet/dry vacuum. Some sort of table saw. Planks of sawed-off two-by-fours and large pieces of plywood leaning against a far corner.

The rest of the room appeared to be empty . . . except for the ancient-looking, arched-stone doorway that appeared in the wall opposite where they'd entered.

Stella directed the flashlight at the door's wide wood planks. Rusted nail heads were as big as coins. There was no handle, only an iron ring hanging from a hasp like an old-fashioned door knocker.

"This has *got* to lead to one of the rooms Gordon mentioned." When Alex stepped closer, a strange sensation sparked in his forehead, a hint of a headache that felt like a warning.

"Alex," Stella whispered unsurely, but when he lifted the ring and gave it a tug, the door held steady. He tried pushing, but that didn't work either.

"Must be bolted from the other side."

"How can that be? Someone locked themself in the room? And then just . . . stayed there?"

"There's got to be another way in. From the north wing, maybe. Charlie probably knows."

"We can't ask him, obviously," Stella said. "Should we get out of here?"

That twinge in Alex's forehead came again. "Hold on." He stepped closer to the door. There were crevices between the planks. He brought his face up to them and tried to peer through. The gaps weren't wide enough for the flashlight. He pressed his ear to the wood and heard an emptiness, almost like the rushing noise that comes when you listen to a spiral shell at the beach. If he let his mind go blurry, it was almost like a tune.

The tune that Simon had said the ghost girl was singing. But there was no ghost girl . . .

"Alex?"

He jolted, knocking into the door, rattling the hinges and the iron ring.

Stella was looking at him with a funny expression. "You hear anything?"

"Nope," Alex lied. "Nothing at all."

Back upstairs, he had just managed to close the basement door when Simon peeked his head over the banister above. "What are you two doing?"

"Not much," said Alex. "Just . . . looking around."

"*Looking around?*" Simon echoed skeptically.

"What are *you* doing?" Stella asked, changing the subject like a boss.

"I was just talking with Zachary." Simon shrugged. "Do you guys want to watch TV?"

"We're grounded, remember?" Alex answered, more harshly than he meant to. "No TV. No phone. No computer."

"Dad and Bev won't know."

"That's what you think."

The twins crept down the hallway to Charlie's office. "You know Simon's watching us, right?" Stella whispered. Alex nodded. "We can pretend that we're cleaning."

"Maybe we can bore him to death," Alex said, amused.

Stella called out, just loud enough. "Okay, then, let's just fix up Charlie's office for him." Alex covered his mouth, hiding a laugh.

They snuck inside, and then closed the door. "There's got to be floor plans in here somewhere," Alex said. "I saw Charlie looking at them a few days ago."

"Were they new? Or the ones for the original building?"

"Both? Maybe? Either way, I'm sure they'll show us how to get into that room downstairs."

"Where we can turn on all the lights." This had become Stella's mantra.

They went through Charlie's desk drawers and the shelves lining the walls. They searched through filing cabinets, opening slim folders with paperwork inside.

"I don't think it's here," Stella said.

Hours later, they'd scoured much of the living space. They'd gone through Mom and Charlie's bedroom. They'd looked in the den, the kitchen, and the bathrooms. They even went out to Charlie's pickup and peered through the windows.

Stella groaned as if she were suddenly ill. "*Alex* . . . What if, this whole time, they've had the plans with them?"

"There's still one place we haven't looked," Alex said. Stella scrunched her brow. He nodded across the gravel lot to the low building on the other side — the long shed that Charlie had mentioned wanting to turn into a garage.

The sun was getting low. There wasn't much time left before Charlie and Mom finished for the day.

The twins dashed to the building. The side door was so

flimsy, it didn't shut properly. They slipped inside. Though the space wasn't particularly dark, it swirled with dust, so Stella switched on the flashlight again. When she swept the beam around, Alex spotted his stepfather's worktable.

Rushing over, they found stacks of blueprints. One for each wing of the old school. "Wow," Alex whispered. "This is it." He and Stella high-fived. "Took us long enough!"

Charlie had placed small stones on each corner to keep the pages from curling up.

"The pages are huge," Stella said. "We can't just *take* them. Mom and Charlie would murder us. Could we snap a pic?"

"Mom still has our phone, but we don't need it. And we don't need the pages either." When Stella threw him a puzzled look, Alex added, "Think you might be able to make some quick copies?"

Stella grinned. "I'll grab my sketchbook."

When she returned, Alex had just begun to make sense of the plans. Stella pulled up a stool next to the table, took the pencil from behind her ear, and got to work.

By the time she'd copied most of the plans into her book, Alex noticed that the buzz saw and hammering coming from the south wing had stopped. "Stell, we gotta go," he said.

Once back inside, they rushed down the hall to the den at the back of the house.

The front door opened behind them.

Stella turned on the standing lamp and tossed her feet up onto the coffee table.

Charlie bellowed, "Phew, I need a shower!"

Within seconds, Mom peeked her head through the doorway. "What are you feeling for dinner? I was thinking burgers and macaroni salad."

"That sounds *dee-lish*," said Alex, pretending to be engrossed in a home decor magazine.

"Need any help?" asked Stella.

"When everything is almost ready, you can ask Simon to join you in setting the table."

As soon as their mother was gone, Alex reached for Stella's notebook and opened to the new pages. "When can we start?"

"Not tonight, obviously. I'm not wandering around in the dark."

"After school tomorrow, then."

Stella shook her head. "Mom and Charlie haven't stopped working until way late every day."

"Isn't there another town meeting this week? Maybe they'll be out."

"We might have to wait until next weekend before we get a chance to explore the north wing."

"That stinks!" said Alex.

Stella bit at her lip for a moment, before suddenly perking up. "Didn't Gordon say your math teacher used to work here?" Alex nodded. "We definitely don't have to wait a week to talk to him."

CHAPTER NINETEEN
ALEX

THE NEXT DAY, at the start of lunch, Alex met Stella at the water fountain near the end of the sixth grade hallway. "You're sure this is when he's at his desk?" she asked.

"He told me so this morning."

"And he doesn't mind that we just barge in and talk to him?"

"Well, it would probably be a good idea to knock first."

Stella made a face, and they headed toward Mr. Levinthal's office. Stella looked jumpy, and her racing voice gave away her nerves. "I can't believe he agreed to just spill the beans about his time at Wildwyck. I mean, I heard he was pretty tough."

Alex swallowed. "The thing is . . . I didn't really mention what it was we wanted to talk about."

"Oh." Stella's face fell. "So, for all he knows, you're heading in to ask about the square root of pi?"

"The square *what* of *what*?"

"Never mind." She stopped short, her shoes sending squeals as they braked against the tile floor. Alex threw her a look that asked, *What's with you?* She nodded at the open door. "He probably heard everything we just said," she whispered. "You go first."

When Alex knocked, Mr. Levinthal glanced up from his desk by the window. "Hello, Mr. Hill. Come on in."

Alex was surprised to find that some of Stella's anxiety had rubbed off. "H-Hi, Mr. L. Um, I hope you don't mind, I brought my twin sister, Stella."

"I see," said Mr. Levinthal, curiously. "Do twins always travel in pairs?"

"Not always," Stella answered politely.

Mr. Levinthal smiled, then tilted his head toward Alex. "What's this all about? I've got quite a few quizzes to grade before the next bell."

"Sorry, it's just . . . Well . . . We've heard . . . You used to teach at Wildwyck School?"

Mr. Levinthal pressed his lips together tightly. "A long time ago. Yes." A slight crease bent his brow. "Who told you that?"

"Our friend Gordon Weinberger," said Stella. "He goes to school here too."

"I don't know him." Mr. Levinthal lifted his shoulders. "Apparently, he knows me."

"I think it's more that he knows Wildwyck," Alex went on. "He's kind of a geek about it. See, I'm not sure if you've heard, but our parents bought the old school building. We've been living there since July."

The teacher sat back in his chair. "Actually, I hadn't heard that." Alex studied Mr. Levinthal's face. Was he telling the truth? What would it mean if he wasn't?

Stella tried, her voice practically a squeak, "We were wondering if you could tell us anything about your time there?"

"I could probably write a book about it," Mr. Levinthal answered slowly, thoughtfully. "What do you want to know? *Anything* is a huge topic, and uh . . ." He pointed to his bare wrist. "Clock's ticking."

Stella's eyes went wide as she blurted, "How'd you get the job? How long did you work there? Where did you live? What were the students like? Did you know Hart and Ada Wildwyck? Why did you leave? Who was — "

Mr. Levinthal held up a hand like a stop sign. "Like I said, *anything* is a big topic."

Stella turned crimson. "Sorry. I guess, you could start with those, and then — "

"And then the period will be over." The teacher gave a sad glance at his unmarked papers, then rolled his eyes. He gestured to the two closest desks. "You have five minutes."

Alex felt both excited and strange. Shouldn't Mr. Levinthal have been intrigued that one of his new students lived in the building where he used to work? More than five minutes' worth?

"The basics," said Mr. Levinthal. Alex wanted to take out a notebook and pen, but he was worried his teacher might think that was weird. So he folded his hands and listened. "It was late summer, 1974. I had just graduated from college. Hart Wildwyck interviewed me. Told me on the spot the job was mine if I wanted it. There was housing on campus for staff and faculty. My parents lived a couple towns over from Frost Meadow, so I figured it would be a good place to start. It was a perk to be able to have a home-cooked meal every weekend. A nice break from cheese sandwiches and canned tomato soup."

Alex squeezed at his own fingers. *Clock's ticking*, he thought. "Where was the housing?" he asked.

"There were a few cottages just north of the main building, across the field. I'm pretty sure they've fallen into disrepair. A fire maybe? Or a storm? My co-workers and I each had our own room, but we shared the common areas, the kitchen, and the bath." He paused, looking inward, remembering. "It was a good group. Every one of us wanted to do our best to help the boys."

"So, you, like, *liked* the students?" Stella asked again, her cheeks turning pink.

"Liked them, of course." Mr. Levinthal smirked. "They were characters. The school had a reputation, but it was mostly mythology. 'Bad boys from the big city. Troublemakers.' But the truth was, those kids wanted to be there. Most of them believed we were their best chance at — " He paused, caught his breath, examined his fingernails. "Well . . . at helping them become who they wished to be."

"You taught there for a long time?" Alex thought to say.

Mr. Levinthal sniffed, sounding almost offended. "Barely a year."

"Did you get fired?" Stella asked brusquely. Alex noticed that she was squeezing her fingers in her lap. Her nerves were getting to her.

A weird expression came across the teacher's face. Suspicion? Maybe they were grilling him too hard. Alex let out a laugh, hoping to soften the sudden tension. "We're just curious why you left."

"*Just curious*," Mr. Levinthal echoed. "Well, you do live

there, after all. To answer your question, no, I was not fired."
He paused, as if trying to quickly put together some puzzle
pieces that the twins couldn't see. Stella opened her mouth to
respond, but all that came out was a sudden coughing fit. The
teacher squinted, then leaned forward, his stomach pressing
against the desk, catching his tie, stretching it tight. "What's
this *really* about?" he asked.

Alex felt his muscles tense. Mr. Levinthal glanced back
and forth between the twins. "Did you know Margaret
Wildwyck?" Alex blurted out.

Mr. Levinthal went pale.

Stella kicked over her book bag. "Shoot," she whispered
before removing the metal box she'd brought from home.
Opening the lid, she took out the Polaroid of the girl. She
froze, holding it only halfway toward Mr. Levinthal, before
she started to tremble.

Alex grabbed the picture and placed it on the desk. "Is
this Margaret?" he asked.

"Maybe we could talk more if your parents — " Looking
closer, Mr. Levinthal contemplated the girl's face before flipping the Polaroid over. He scanned the inscription. *P. ~1975.*
Something behind his eyes seemed to soften. "Yes, actually,"
he said.

"Why would someone have written the letter *P* here?"

"I'd assume it was because people called her Peggy. A
nickname for Margaret. Strange, I know. Like Teddy for
Edward. Or Jack for John. Doesn't make much sense."

"And 1975?" Stella pressed suddenly, as if to make up for
her earlier shakiness. "This was taken just before she died?"

Alex felt numb. He didn't want to bring up her death just yet.

"I wouldn't know." Mr. Levinthal stood with finality. "I've really got to get back to grading."

Alex grabbed the edges of his desk. "But Mr. Levinthal —"

"I'll see you kids around." He looked toward the hallway. "Close the door, would you?"

CHAPTER TWENTY
STELLA

On the bus ride home, neither twin mentioned what they'd learned. They didn't want to risk Simon hearing them and then blurting out something stupid about it for the whole bus to hear. Even though Simon was sitting a few rows ahead with one of his new groupies, they couldn't trust him. He had ears like a cat — it seemed they could swivel and pay attention to two things at once. The only thing Stella said about it was, "I can't believe how badly I messed that up."

"You didn't mess up anything," Alex said, unsure if he believed himself. "Mr. Levinthal just ran out of time is all."

In the kitchen, they found Mom at the table, looking over some paperwork. She'd already laid out apple slices and had smothered them with peanut butter. The kids swarmed the plate. Stella had just bitten into her first slice — apple juice dribbling past her lips, peanut butter sticking to the roof of her mouth — when she noticed a book sitting on the table. *Frost Meadow: A History*. She'd never seen this before. A paper receipt had been shoved between the pages and was sticking out from the top. Stella read the name of the store where her mother must have bought it. *Our Book Shop*.

She'd noticed the bookstore in the village whenever the family had driven through, but she hadn't gone inside yet. She had almost a full case of books in her room that she still needed to work through. She finished chewing, wiped her hands, and then picked up the slim volume. There were old photographs and paintings on every page — images of what the village had looked like throughout the centuries.

"Isn't that great?" said Mom. Stella handed the book to Alex, who'd been peering over her shoulder. "I bought it this morning. Thought it would be fun to look through. There are even a few pages about the old Wildwyck School. Did you know there used to be cottages across the field, over by the woods?"

"Actually . . . We *did* know that," Stella said.

"Can I see?" said Simon, grabbing the book from Alex, who looked suddenly like he might start fuming out the ears. "Does it mention anything about ghosts?"

Mom stiffened, but smiled. "I haven't gotten a chance to read through the whole thing yet. But . . . *maybe?*"

"Cool!" said Simon, running down the hall to the den, taking the book with him.

Stella bit back her annoyance and grabbed another slice of peanut-butter-apple.

"I met the shop owner too," Mom went on. "Nice guy. Name's Ship Curtis. We got to talking, and it turns out, he was a student here, a long time ago."

"Here?" Alex repeated. "At Wildwyck?"

"Isn't that funny? Said his family lived in the area. They thought he'd get a better education at the boys' school than at the public school. He told me that when he graduated, he took over his parents' bookstore. He's been in Frost Meadow forever." Mom gave herself a soft squeeze. "I love stories like this!"

"That's awesome, Mom," said Alex. "We've got lots of homework, so we'll see you later." He started toward the staircase. "Thanks for the snack!"

"Don't forget you're still grounded. So, no internet. No phones. No *games*."

"Got it," said Stella, following Alex upstairs. She wondered what her mother would say if she knew what they'd done with Charlie's floor plans, or what they intended to do with them when she wasn't looking. It wasn't a game, exactly, but she knew her mom wouldn't approve.

CHAPTER TWENTY-ONE
ZACHARY

September 9

It's not fair!

What happened wasn't my fault and Dad and Bev won't believe me. They say they don't want me hanging out with my new friends anymore. And worse, they say that if something like this happens again, they'll send me away.

Away? What does that even mean?

Yesterday, I was with Joshua after school. We were walking around Frost Meadow, taking turns on his skateboard.

Before I realize, we're at the shopping plaza just outside the village. There's a TJ Maxx and Joshua really wants to go in, so I follow him. My mom sent me some spending money, and I figure maybe I could find a cool T-shirt or something.

So we're going around the store and I notice that Joshua's, like, sticking stuff in his pockets. Like, MERCHANDISE. And I ask him what he's thinking and he says It's just a little fun.

Just a little fun.

And he picks up this leather bracelet and puts it on my wrist, and then holds his finger up to his lips like to say shh, only he didn't say shh. And I roll my eyes and laugh, because like yeah, right, I'm actually going to steal this garbage? No. But he walks off and keeps doing what he's doing.

I ignore him and go over to the racks and I find a couple of cool weird shirts that happen to be my size, so I decide to get them. Also, Mom told me she wanted me to find a new pair of sneakers and there's this whole sneaker section so I try on a wild-looking pair of Nikes and they fit and I decide to get those too.

As I get to the cashier, Joshua comes up beside me, which makes me really nervous, because I have no idea how many things are in his pockets at this point. So I take out my money and I pay for my shirts and my shoes and Joshua and me head out the front door and the next thing I know, there's a security guard blocking our path, saying, I'm going to need you two to come with me.

I wanted to die!

I followed the guard to an office at the back of the store, sure that I'd done nothing wrong, that clearly everyone had seen ME pay for my items and even if they hadn't, I had a receipt in my bag, but then the guard sits us down and tells Joshua to empty his pockets.

And then he points to my wrist, where that DUMB leather bracelet is still tied. I'd completely forgotten about it. And I'd tried to walk out of the store with it!

In conclusion: He said that I SHOPLIFTED.

But I'd just paid like over fifty bucks for all my stuff. Why would I have tried to steal something worth another five dollars? I said that to the guard but he shrugged. Joshua looked like a turtle who wanted to pull his head inside his shell.

The ACTUAL cops show up. They put us in ACTUAL handcuffs, sit us in the back of the cruiser, then take us to ACTUAL JAIL.

The next thing I know, Dad and Bev are there and they look scared and furious, if that's even a thing – fear-fury? – and the cops let me out and I sit in the back seat and no one speaks the whole way to Wildwyck.

Later, I tried to explain to them what had happened. That it was all just a misunderstanding, that Joshua's never even done anything like that before, and you know what they said? They said I was LYING. That I knew exactly what I was doing when I wore that bracelet out of the store. And no matter how I answered, they wouldn't believe me. So now, I can't hang out with my best friend, or any of his friends, including Peggy, who I think I really like – like a lot – and I mean what's the point of even staying here anymore?

If I tell the truth and no one believes me, why shouldn't I just start lying more often?

Or like all the time?

Simon does it. Alex does it. Stella too. And all they get is their phone taken away. What kind of punishment is that? It's not like it's stopped them from fighting for two straight months. They hate each other at this point. They've all told me so. Simon hates Alex and Stella. Alex hates Simon. Stella...Well, who knows what her deal is? She's just like Simon said: a horse girl with a horsey face. A loser.

On top of everything else, I overheard Bev and my dad talking about actual DIVORCE!

And Simon just won't stop with the ghost stories, whether they're true or not. Whether he even believes them or not. My brother is a little devil who wants to destroy everything that's good because it amuses him. He's a pathetic speck of fecality.

Yet I'M the one being turned into a monster. I'M the bad guy? Because of one mistake? One mistake is all it takes?

Fine.

Dad and Bev want a bad guy? I can be a bad guy. I can be the BEST bad guy. They have no idea.

Simon and the twins want a ghost in this house? I'll give them a ghost. Let's see if any of them ever sleep again.

Your friend,

Z

CHAPTER TWENTY-TWO
SIMON

ALEX AND STELLA had thought they'd been super sneaky, but Simon knew what was up. They'd been ghost hunting. Actual ghost hunting, the entire week, and they hadn't included him. They'd made that new friend, Gordon, who they treated more like a brother than they'd ever treated him. Now it was Saturday, and they were about to do their most daring feat yet, and they'd said nothing to him about it. Absolutely nothing . . .

He was the spooky kid. *He* was the one who liked ghost stories! *He* was the one who paid attention to the things that other people ignored. Not them. *Not them!*

Simon felt angry. More than angry. He wasn't even really sure what to call the thing he was feeling. Whatever this new emotion was, it crept through his skin and made his head feel swimmy. He wished he could vent to Zachary. He was certain Zachary would help talk him down. But for the past couple days, Zachary hadn't felt like talking, and Simon wondered if somehow the twins had gotten to him as well, which only made his skin feel creepier and his head even swimmier.

This made Simon want to do bad things.

So, late Saturday afternoon, Simon watched from afar as they continued their plan to break into one of the forbidden wings of the house. Dad and Bev had gone into town, looking for a particular tool, so the twins finally felt like they were free to explore the old building.

The low sun was making shadows reach long across the fields.

"Are you sure this is the right key?" Stella asked, standing at the door near the back part of the north wing. Alex was struggling to open a padlock Charlie had bolted to a flimsy piece of plywood.

Simon watched from around the corner.

"Yes, I'm sure." Alex turned the key back and forth. "It's just . . . finicky." The lock clicked open. "See? Told ya."

"You sure did."

Last weekend, they'd talked about all this up in the barn with Gordon. Simon hadn't told anyone about falling into the sunken cistern. He *could* have scared the twins with that story — seeing the silhouette, hearing the laughter and the growl — could have made Stella look over her shoulder more than usual, but he'd chosen not to. He'd believed in the connection they'd made that day, that they might finally begin seeing him as an actual brother and not a nuisance.

Why didn't they want his help?

Alex swung open the plywood panel and slipped inside with Stella. Simon waited for a few seconds, then rushed to the door.

Their voices echoed.

"The map says we head this way," said Stella.

"You're the boss."

"I'm not the boss. I'm your sister."

"Fine. Then, *I'm* the boss."

Stella let out a groan. She didn't seem to be frightened at all. Simon smiled. Should she be, maybe? A little bit?

Silently, he squeezed through the gap in the entry, careful to not touch the plywood. He couldn't risk making the hinges squeal. He found himself inside a mudroom. Through the doorway just ahead, he noticed a beam of light reflecting off some distant wall. He peered around the corner to see the twins disappear through an archway.

He crept onward. Most of the windows on the ground level had been boarded up, so there was very little light to see by. He'd have to stay close to the twins' flashlight if he didn't want to vanish in the darkness.

This area looked like it had been classrooms. Dark doorways opened on either side of the hall. The checkered linoleum floor had been worn down to the wood beneath it. Pieces of plaster and paint chips had rained down from the ceiling and were scattered across his path. He was careful to not step on anything in case a crunch gave him away.

Stella's voice floated out. "The stairway should be just around this bend."

The glow from Stella's flashlight began to fade. Simon picked up the pace. Turning the next corner, he watched the beam bounce downward. At the bottom of the stairs, the twins hesitated before another dark hall. Stella consulted the map. Alex shined the flashlight all around. The ceiling here was low, the floor made of dirt.

"What's that?" Alex said, flinching, then focusing the beam ahead.

"What's *what*?" Stella asked.

Simon could already see what Alex was pointing at. At the far end of the passage, just before the spot where the light couldn't reach, dust motes flurried.

Alex huffed. "It's probably just a draft."

"A draft?" Stella whispered. "From where?"

Simon thought it was funny that they were scared of dust. But then he remembered the silhouette that had laughed at him from the lip of the cistern. What if that same silhouette was watching, standing beyond the flashlight's glow?

"Come on," said Alex, walking forward. "You said it was this way?"

Holding her notebook out before herself, Stella swallowed hard. "Right."

The two wandered. Shadows followed closely. Simon felt dizzy. It was darker down here than it had been upstairs — no daylight seeping in. He held his breath as he tiptoed through the shadows that lengthened between the twins and himself. He paused as they stopped before the swirling dust motes. When Stella reached out a hand, she chuckled. She pointed to a hole in the wall near the ceiling. "Draft's coming in from up there."

"Nothing to be scared of," Alex said.

"I wasn't scared," Stella insisted. Simon could tell she was lying.

They made their way through an opening to their right.

Simon scrambled to catch up. But in the dark, in his panic, he stepped on a loose piece of mortar. It went skittering down the hall.

The twins paused.

"What's that?" Stella asked, unable to hide her alarm.

"A rodent," Alex answered unsurely.

Simon pressed himself against the wall. What would he do if they came back to check? He had nowhere to hide.

"Is that supposed to be reassuring?"

"Better than a ghost . . . Right?"

"I guess."

"The door should be just up here."

Simon moved more slowly up the passage. The idea of a haunting no longer seemed fun. If he didn't have the twins to focus on, he was pretty sure his worry might turn him to stone, down in the depths of the north wing, where none of them was supposed to be, and where no one would likely search. He came to a corner. The twins stood before a wooden door that looked almost exactly like the one Simon had found in their own basement.

"This is just the other side of the same door," Alex said, disappointed.

"But it's not," Stella answered, pointing again to her notebook. "If it were the *same* door, the room we're standing in now would be a giant square just like the floor plan shows. But this room is longer. And the wall on the right is at an angle. I think the square room is just beyond *this* door."

"So then . . . We're still locked out?"

Stella laughed. "Try opening it first?"

"Oh, right!"

Simon clutched at the door frame. This had been a bad idea. A mistake. And not just because if their parents found them, they'd probably all be stuck in their bedrooms for the rest of their lives. Something was down here with them. He could feel it, just like the first time he'd set foot in Wildwyck.

Alex reached for the iron ring. When he pulled it, the door gave way. He yelped, then cheered, jumping up and down.

"Shhh! Simon might hear us! We don't want him down here."

Simon scowled. *Why not?* he wanted to shout. But suddenly, he knew *why not*. He'd been horrible to them. Seeing them down here, relating as brother and sister, helping each other along each creepy step, he understood something he'd never understood before. They got along because they trusted each other.

Trust.

Simon hadn't tried to build it. Not at first. And maybe now he'd never have the chance. They wouldn't let him.

Alex gave the door another hard tug and the ancient hinges squealed.

Stella stepped through the doorway. Alex held up the light. Simon heard her say, "What's all this — "

But then something happened. Something he wasn't able to make out.

Both twins grunted, as if someone had shoved them. He heard them hit the floor. The flashlight flew backward. It rolled out through the doorway toward him.

Simon bolted from his hiding spot to pick up the light. He'd managed to shine it through the doorway to see who was in there with them. Alex lifted his head, holding up his hand, blocking the glare. "Simon? Is that you?" Stella tried to stand, but she faltered and fell again.

"Yeah," Simon said. "But I'm here to — "

The door slammed shut. Simon hadn't been near it. He froze, holding the flashlight like a weapon, too frightened to move.

The twins were screaming now, their voices muffled behind the door.

Simon swiveled, scanning the darkness around him. He ran to the door and grabbed at the ring. But now it wouldn't open. "Let go of the handle!" he shouted. But the twins were too frantic to hear him. "It's stuck! Let go! I need to pull from *this* side!"

"Simon!" Alex called out, a fury in his voice that could have sparked a fire. "Let us out!"

Angry tears flooded behind Simon's eyes. They were blaming him for this? "I'm trying! You need to let go of the door!"

Stella called back through wavering sobs. "W-We're not t-touching the door!"

Simon stepped back, shining the light at the stone archway, looking for a place where the wood might have gotten caught on the stone archway.

Alex raged, "I'm going to get you for this!"

"I didn't . . . It's not me . . ."

"Simon," said Stella. She'd somehow managed to find a bit of calm. "Listen to me. We're not mad. Just please. Let us out. It's not funny."

Simon was not laughing. "Don't be scared," he answered. "I'm going to find help."

CHAPTER TWENTY-THREE
SIMON

HE RACED THROUGH the darkened corridors, holding a scream just at the back of his throat.

Every door that appeared seemed like the one he should take, but Simon knew if he made a wrong turn, he'd be lost down here, as hopeless as the twins trapped in that room back there. They'd thought he was playing a prank. Could they really believe he was that cruel?

He paused where three openings led to who-knew-where and shone the light through each portal. Just beyond the arch on the left, footprints marked the dust, patterns he recognized from the bottoms of Alex's sneakers. He let out a shaky breath.

This would be his path of bread crumbs, showing the way out. Up the stairs, down the hall, around the bend. His footfalls echoed, making it sound like someone was chasing him. He reached the plywood plank Alex had unlocked and threw it wide open, stepping out into the fading daylight. He wanted to cry out, *Help!* But who would answer? Dad and Bev weren't home. Their neighbors weren't close enough to hear him. He could try tracking down Zachary, but what good would that do?

Simon tore around the side of the north wing. The

courtyard appeared, surrounded by the gravel drive. To his surprise, he heard the sound of an engine approaching.

A moment later, his dad's pickup came flying up the road, trailing a cloud of dirt. Simon dashed onto the lawn and waved his hands over his head. The truck coughed to a stop. Bev leapt from the passenger side. Simon realized for the first time that he was covered with dust, his face caked with a mix of dirt and tears. "What is it, Simon? What's wrong?" Bev asked.

"Promise you won't be mad."

When his father came around the front of the truck, the look he wore said that no promises would be made or kept. "Where are they?"

Simon led his parents sheepishly around the back side of the north wing. Bev saw the plywood door swinging in the breeze and she let out a small cry.

Simon tracked the footprints back down to the basement. Now that his dad and Bev were with him, the place felt less threatening, the shadows brighter, the echoes less clamoring, as if the anger of parents could keep back the things that thrive in the dark. In the basement, Dad and Bev followed the cries of the twins. With their every shout, Simon cringed, even though, this time, he knew it wasn't his fault. Dad and Bev came to the room with the door. Dad grabbed the flash-light from Simon's hand so quickly, Simon almost screamed himself.

Bev called out, "Stella! Alex!"

"Mom! We're in here!"

Bev grabbed at the iron ring and pulled, but the door could have been made of steel.

Dad looked at Simon, a mix of exhaustion and anger swarming his face. "What did you do?"

"Nothing! I swear."

Bev held his arm. "Charlie, please. Just . . . help me with this. They really are locked in."

Simon flushed. He felt empty. They didn't believe him. Of course, they didn't. He'd given them no reason to do so.

Dad called out to the twins, "Kids, step back from the door."

"You'll hurt yourself," Bev warned.

Dad hurtled forward and rammed the wood. A great cracking echoed through the space. Simon wasn't sure if it had come from wood or if it had been bone. From beyond, the twins shrieked. Dad stumbled backward, clutching at his shoulder.

"You all right?" Bev asked.

"Darn thing is solid."

"Hold on a few more seconds," Bev said at the door. "Charlie's gonna get you out." What Simon heard was *Because your stepbrother was dumb enough to lock you in.*

Dad kicked at the wood. With wild energy, he managed to pull pieces of it apart, giant rusted nail heads tumbling to the dirt below. Seconds later, Stella and Alex stumbled out of the darkness, their faces flushed and streaked with red. Bev held them both tightly as all three sobbed. Dad had already stepped aside, observing the huddle with a worried expression, holding the flashlight toward the ground so that no one would be blinded by the beam.

Simon felt invisible again. Then Alex looked past his mother to where he stood, arms wrapped around himself.

Alex lunged, reaching toward Simon. "YOU!" he growled.

CHAPTER TWENTY-FOUR
ALEX

CHARLIE STEPPED BETWEEN the boys. "Okay, okay," he said, struggling to pull Alex away. "Stop it, Alex!" He threw a glance to Mom, as if only she were capable of quieting him.

She came up from behind Alex and clutched his shoulders. He stopped fighting.

Charlie looked to all of them. "Someone better start explaining things real fast."

Alex's brain felt like grilled cheese: completely melted. "Simon followed Stella and me down here. He pushed us into this room, knocked us down, stole our flashlight, and then locked the door."

"That's not true!" Simon yelled. "I followed them, yes, but I didn't hurt them. And I didn't shut the door. That happened on its own."

Charlie threw his hands in the air. "Enough with the ghost nonsense, Simon!"

"It's not nonsense! I'm telling the truth. Why would I have done that, then rushed upstairs to tell you?"

"I don't know why you do *most* of what you do," Charlie answered. "You're acting like . . . someone I don't even know anymore."

"*Charlie*," Bev said in a hushed tone.

"All right." Flustered, Charlie turned to the twins. "If

Simon's telling the truth, why would you two have thought it a good idea to steal my key, open the lock, and start exploring?"

Alex sighed, finding his breath, searching for actual words. "I know . . . Th-This looks bad." Charlie and Mom both raised their eyebrows. "Okay. An understatement. B-But, we had a good reason." He glanced at his sister, who'd moved as far away from the broken door as possible. "Stella's been having a hard time. She . . . she's been scared." Stella covered her face. He glared at Simon. "Mostly, I think, because of all the ridiculous stories Simon's been telling. About ghosts and shadows and humming and . . . and that *growling*."

"They're not just stories. You heard it too."

Alex stomped his foot, and Simon clamped his mouth shut. Mom clutched his shoulders tighter as if that would keep him in place. "We came up with this plan. We thought that if we could figure out what happened here at Wildwyck, everything would seem . . . less weird."

Stella spoke up. "We wanted to turn on all the lights."

"*Turn on all the lights?*" Mom echoed.

"Like, to get rid of the shadows. So we could see the truth. And not be scared."

Charlie shook his head. "I don't understand."

"We learned things this week," said Alex. "Things about the people who used to live here."

"*What* people?" Mom asked.

Alex turned to face her. "There was a girl. The daughter of the headmaster. Her name was Margaret, but everyone called her Peggy."

"She died," Stella added. "Way back in the 1970s."

"Who told you this?" Mom asked.

Alex and Stella told them about their conversation with Mr. Levinthal.

"We found her grave in the woods, out behind the barn," Alex added. "In the Wildwyck family plot." The twins shared everything that they'd learned. They told the others how their new friend Gordon had filled in some of the blanks, and how all of them had discovered a metal box in the barn the previous weekend. Stella talked about the water-damaged journal and the Polaroid of Peggy. Alex mentioned the punishment rooms that Gordon had told them about. All the while, Alex noticed Simon standing off to the side, listening, looking sad, but that must have only been from the shadows.

Charlie cleared his throat. "That is . . . a whole lot." He swung the flashlight toward the shattered remains of the door. "But why come down here? What were you looking for?"

"We thought the Liars' Room might have been behind the door in *our* basement. We were looking for another way in. We wanted to see . . . if there was anything more we could learn from looking inside."

"Turn on all the lights?" Mom repeated.

"Exactly," Alex answered.

"And did you?" Charlie asked. "Learn anything?"

Stella stepped closer to the doorway. "It was too dark. We were scared. But right before . . ." Her eyes swung toward Simon. "Right before the door slammed shut, I thought I saw . . . I don't know. It looked like there was . . . *writing* . . . on the walls."

Charlie squinted. He held out his hand as if to protect the others, then stepped over the debris and through the stone arch. After a few seconds, he shouted, "Simon! Get in here. Now!"

Chapter Twenty-Five
Stella

STELLA PRESSED HERSELF against the wall and watched as Simon made his way cautiously toward the broken door. The flashlight beam darted around inside, illuminating sections of the dark room. Her heart thumped. Though she couldn't read it from here, it was clear now that she'd been right — someone had marked bold white letters, numbers, and words across nearly every wall.

Charlie's voice came from the shadows. "What's all this supposed to mean?"

"I have no idea," Simon said. "I didn't write any of it. How could I? The door was locked."

"Not from this side apparently."

"Dad, I'm not lying. I swear."

Charlie called out. "Bev?"

Mom glanced at the twins, then waved them nervously toward her. Together, the three passed through the doorway. The smell struck Stella, nearly knocked her off her feet. It wasn't bad but powerful — it made her think of the inky dark that had surrounded her and Alex and how desperate she'd felt as she had screamed with him for help. Mold, earth . . . and chalk?

Charlie held the beam steady so they could all read the writing.

"August 17 . . . These have been some strange days. I blame my little brother. Simon is a pretty sensitive kid, which is one of the reasons we share the attic bedroom here at Wildwyck. It's the biggest room in the house, so we have plenty of space to ourselves, but Simon doesn't like to be alone, not at night . . ."

A journal entry.

"I don't understand," Stella said. "Simon doesn't share the attic bedroom with anyone. Who wrote this?"

"Little brother," Alex whispered.

And then Stella understood. Or at least she thought she did. She looked to the end of this first section, near the signature, and read aloud: *"I'm not sure what to believe anymore, especially if it comes out of Simon's mouth. I'll have to ask Joshua and Peggy the next time we all hang out if anyone has ever seen ghosts at Wildwyck and if I should be worried. Your friend, Zachary Kidd."*

Zachary. Simon's older brother.

"But Zachary couldn't have written this," Stella went on.

"Obviously," Alex said, glaring at Simon. "He lives in Ohio. With his mother."

There was a terrible moment of silence. Stella turned to look at Simon and felt her mother and Charlie do the same beside her.

"Why are you all looking at me?" Simon asked. "I didn't do this. I *couldn't* have done this."

"Well, someone did it," Charlie answered. "And it sure wasn't Bev or me."

Stella glanced at some of the other entries. She read names

like Joshua and Peggy. Passages leapt out at her. *"Good for them if the therapist is helping. That's what they do, right? Help? But the fact that they're lying about it to us might mean it's not."*

And, *"The most effective lies are the ones that have a seed of truth inside them."*

And, *"Bev was going on and on about Simon and how she thought he was a bad influence on the twins. And then Dad chimes in and says that the twins aren't any better."*

And, *"If I tell the truth and no one believes me, why shouldn't I just start lying more often? Or, like, all the time?"*

And, *"Simon hates Alex and Stella. Alex hates Simon. Stella . . . Well, who knows what her deal is? She's just like Simon said: a horse girl with a horsey face. A loser."*

And worst of all, *"On top of everything else, I overheard Bev and my dad talking about actual DIVORCE!"*

Mom's eyes flicked back and forth between the twins and Simon. "Let's get them out of here."

Charlie grunted. He was reading the same passages.

Were they true? Did everyone in the family hate everyone else? Were Charlie and Mom really talking about getting a divorce? About leaving Wildwyck and all that they'd struggled so hard to accomplish?

"Charlie!" Mom said again. "Now! I don't want them seeing this . . ."

Charlie jolted out of his stupor. He shone the light at the door on the opposite wall, the one that should lead back to the basement in the center building. He went over and gave it a kick. The door swung open with ease.

*   *   *

Upstairs, Charlie and Mom asked the three kids to sit in the den while they spoke in the kitchen.

Charlie had instructed, "No talking until we get back. I don't want to hear *one word.*" Stella had almost expected Simon to say something like, *What about two words?* But he'd only stared at his father with wide, puzzled eyes.

Of course, Stella knew you don't need language to tell a lie.

She sat quietly on the leather couch, unable to control her tears. She was confused.

Hurt.

Was Simon really that foolish?

Was foolish even the correct word?

Another idea materialized.

Could it have been *Alex*?

Had he set up their stepbrother, knowing that when Mom and Charlie discovered the writing, Simon would be the obvious culprit? Alex had been the one who'd had the idea to look for the door to the secret room. What if he'd spent the whole week sneaking down there, through the passage in the north wing, using chalk to write on the walls? What if he was the one who'd orchestrated them finding the room, trapping them inside, ensuring that Simon would follow them, rescue them?

What word would describe someone who did *that*?

Disturbed?

Demented?

Unhinged?

Were you even allowed to say those things about a *kid*?

Stella glanced up at her twin, who sat on the edge of the fireplace, his face in his hands. If he *had* done this — to spite their stepbrother and get him in trouble — was it possible that she had never known him? If she didn't know Alex, how could she ever know *anyone at all*?

Simon was picking at the skin on his thumb, mumbling to himself.

Alex whispered, "Your father told us to not talk."

Stella scowled at him, but Alex didn't notice.

Simon's jaw jutted forward. He answered in a louder whisper, "*You're* talking."

"Yeah, but only because *you* — "

"Stop it." Stella didn't want to hear him. "What were you saying, Simon?"

"I was saying how mean it is that someone would pretend to be Zachary. To pretend he wrote those things." Simon glared at Alex. "My brother *loves* me. You don't know. He'd never call me a *faker*. He'd never say he wanted to *kick me*."

Alex shrugged. "If you think it's so mean, then why'd you do it?"

"I didn't!" Simon's eyes nearly popped out.

"Shh!" Stella looked down the hall toward the kitchen, where her mom and Charlie were still talking.

"If you didn't," Alex went on, "then who did?"

"Maybe it was *you*," Stella blurted out. Her face instantly turned red.

"Me? Why would I?"

"To hurt Simon. To . . . mess things up for him. For all of us."

Now Alex was the one who looked hurt. But she didn't care. Or maybe she did. She wasn't sure what to feel or what to believe. "Stella, I would never — "

"Neither would *I*," Simon spoke up.

Stella shook her head. They all knew he totally *would*. He ignored her. "What about all the stuff about 'Zachary' being friends with Peggy?"

Alex leaned toward Simon. "You tried to convince us she's haunting this place."

"And what if — "

"Don't say it."

"But what if she is?" Simon suggested. "What if . . . What if a . . . Her *ghost* wrote all that stuff in the basement?" Alex scoffed, amused but also *not*. "To hurt us, like Stella said. To mess things up. For our family."

"Family?" Alex echoed. "Since when have you cared about our *family*?"

Simon shook his head. "Since . . . since, I don't know when. Since I realized how badly I've screwed everything up."

Stella exhaled slowly, trying to control the wobble she felt in her chest. "I believe you, Simon." She wasn't sure why she said it. She wasn't sure it was even true. Mostly, she wanted to see what Alex's reaction would be. He looked like she'd slapped his face.

"You believe him?"

"Alex, don't."

"After everything I've done? After trying to help you not feel scared here anymore? How could you say that, Stella?"

"I . . . I believe you too," she answered, lifting her chin.

"You can't believe both of us," said Simon.

She crossed her arms, fell back against the couch cushions. "If I believe in ghosts, I can believe in anything."

Simon's eyes lit with surprise.

"I give up," Alex said.

Footsteps were coming down the hallway. Mom appeared in the doorway. "Simon, we called your mother and told her what was going on. She was not pleased, to say the least. She was in the middle of something with Zachary but said she'd call back later." Simon looked like she'd stolen his breath away. After a moment, he nodded. Mom went on, "Charlie has gone back down to the basement. He thought it would be best to take photographs of all the writing before we paint over it."

"You can't paint over it!" Alex said, standing. "It's evidence!"

"Evidence of what?" Mom asked.

"Of a haunting," Simon said.

Alex shuddered. "Evidence that Simon is *seriously* messed up."

Mom blinked at him nervously. "I don't want to hear talk like that, Alex. Not from any of you. Understand?"

"Did you reach Zachary?" Simon asked her. "Does *he* know what happened?"

"That's up to your mother. But I'm sure your brother won't be happy about any of this either." She sat on the couch beside Stella. Stella wanted to curl up in her arms, to let her mom's warmth course through her and make her feel safe again. But Mom didn't look like she was in the mood to be touched.

"Charlie and I spoke. We want you all to know that what you read down there . . . wasn't exactly true."

Some of it had certainly seemed like it could be true, Stella thought. One of the sentences she'd read crept up from her memory: *The most effective lies are the ones that have a seed of truth inside them.*

"Charlie and I are seeing a therapist. But we've been doing that since even before the wedding. There's nothing wrong with seeking help. It keeps us going strong. Just like how Dr. Solomon kept you two strong after Dad died. And divorce has not been part of the conversation. We wouldn't lie about that."

Stella looked into her mother's eyes, hoping to see something there she could trust. They looked like how Mom's eyes always looked. Big and brown and full of kindness and love. But did that mean Stella should believe her?

"And all the rest . . . I just don't know. We're going to have to figure out how to deal. To find answers. This is major, no doubt, but we're going to find a solution. I promise." Mom's words sounded like a puzzle in Stella's brain. Nothing was making sense. "What happened today, and everything that led up to it, the sneaking around, the rule breaking, the stories, the lies . . . It cannot happen. Ever again. I mean it. Do you understand?"

Stella nodded. "Yes, Mom. Of course."

"I understand," Simon answered.

Stella glanced at Alex, who simply leaned back and stared at the ceiling, refusing to say another word.

CHAPTER TWENTY-SIX
SIMON

LATER, CHARLIE SENT them to their rooms.

Simon sat by the gabled window in the attic, looking out across the field where the late day washed the land in a brilliant violet blue. His gaze wandered to the stone wall that cut across the grass, and then up to the woods behind the barn. Memories of all the scary happenings since coming to Wildwyck floated through his mind. But he was certain that the ones from today would plant themselves permanently. Once, he would have been happy to continue living by flashlight, telling tales around a campfire back in Ohio with Zachary, having him lean forward to hang on every sentence. Other things felt more important now. He couldn't stop thinking about what Stella and Alex had said they'd been doing — trying to *turn on all the lights*. He'd watched the door slam shut on the twins. Their screaming was like a siren in his brain. It was unbearable remembering how helpless they'd been down there. In the dark.

Simon's computer chimed. He flinched and glanced over at the laptop's dim screen.

There was a message from Zachary: *We need to talk.* Simon took a breath, then moved the cursor to the camera icon. A new window popped up, and he waited for his brother to answer.

On the screen, Zachary's face appeared, washed out by his desk lamp. Behind him, the bedroom was dark, but Simon made out the familiar furniture and the movie posters on Zachary's wall. *The Lost Boys. Monster Squad. Xanadu. The Goonies.* "Mom told me what happened." Zachary stared out at him for several seconds, his expression like a closed door. "What were you thinking?"

"I didn't do it, Zachary."

"And we're all just supposed to believe you? I know you've heard about the Boy Who Cried Wolf."

"I never cried wolf. All the ghost stories I told them were true."

"*All* of them? You sure?"

"I mean . . . Yeah, mostly. I might have added a few details that weren't true *at first*. But then they became true. I swear. The growling? The twins heard it themselves. Right after they shut me inside the basement staircase."

"You're no victim, Simon. What is this? Last year all over again? Frost Meadow was supposed to be a fresh start."

"It has been! I've already made friends at school. People actually like me here."

"But are they the people who count?"

"Count?"

"Your family, Simon. Stella. Alex. Bev. Dad. The people who count. Don't pretend you don't know what I mean."

"*You* count, Zachary. And you're not here."

"So that's why you wrote me into some story on the basement walls? To bring me *there*?"

"How many times do I have to tell you? It wasn't me."

"It was *someone.*"

"Stella thinks that Alex might have — "

"Oh, please . . ."

"No, really! Alex hates me. He might have done it to make me look bad."

"Why?"

"Because I . . . I haven't been the nicest brother to him. Or to Stella."

Zachary smirked. "Go on," he said, as if he were taking pleasure in torturing him.

"I — I made him look bad in front of the principal at school. And for some reason, he thinks I hacked into his phone, but I swear I didn't do that!"

"You must be innocent, as usual."

"I'm . . . I'm *trying*, Zachary. The last few days . . . I could have told them more about what I've seen. But I . . . I didn't want to scare Stella. And today, I actually saved them."

"Funny, 'cause Dad says you were the one who locked them in."

"Dad's wrong!"

"I don't know, Simon. You say you're trying to be better? You've got to be better than *just* better."

"You mean, like you? Mr. Perfect? With your 'gifted' school that was so special, you had to stay in Ohio with Mom?"

"Twist this all you want. I'm used to it."

"It's not fair. They shouldn't have split us up."

"We've spoken almost every day."

"Talking on the computer is not the same, and you know it."

"I'd be happy to take a break."

"No! Zachary . . . I'm sorry."

"I'm not sure you are."

"So I can't even be angry?"

"Simon . . . Of course you can. Cruddy things have happened to us. To you. You can't let your anger turn you into a . . . a creep. You've got to have hope. Trying to stay positive while all this bonkers stuff is going on, well, I think that's the hardest thing any human being can aim for."

"*I'm* a human being."

"Ha. I know you are. You're an amazing human being. When you want to be."

"Zachary . . . Can you please come visit. Soon?"

"I'd like to. But as you know, I've got my special-fancy-genius school to attend. Maybe on the next long weekend."

"Ask Mom . . . Or don't ask Mom. Just . . . I'll figure out the bus schedule and you can — "

"Simon."

"In Columbus. There's got to be a route that — "

"Simon, I'm not going to do that. Can you imagine how scared Mom or Dad or Bev would be if I disappeared for half a day?"

"They'd be scared, but once you got here, they wouldn't be scared anymore."

"They'd be furious. And I thought I already mentioned that making people mad isn't the best thing at the moment."

"Fine . . . But . . . *Come*. Okay? Please?"

Zachary stared into the camera. Simon could almost feel his gaze as if they were in the same room. Together finally.

A step creaked at the top of the stairs. Simon's skin shrunk as he turned, expecting to see the shadow silhouette that had peered down at him from the edge of the cistern. But it was only his father, with Bev close behind. How long had they been listening?

Dad did not look happy. "So now you're plotting to have Zachary run away?"

"Dad, that's not what — "

Dad leaned down to peer into the laptop's camera. "Hi, Zachary," he said, as if he were both happy and annoyed to see his face. "We'll talk later." Zachary was barely able to respond before Dad slammed the lid shut.

"No!"

"Charlie," Bev warned, but Dad waved away her worry.

He removed the cord and picked up the computer. He didn't look angry. Just tired. "I won't have this anymore. You're going to shape up, or you'll have to ship out, buddy. I know it's what you've wanted. Since your mother wasn't able to manage you back in Ohio, and being here doesn't seem to be helping, we think it might be best if we look for an alternative."

"Alternative?"

"Another school. Where you can learn to behave. There are a few options in neighboring states. Religious. Military. Something disciplined. Seems to me, it's what you need."

"Boarding school? But I don't want — "

"You've made it quite clear what you want." Simon glanced at Bev, who only stared at the floor. "What you did today . . . You need help, Simon. Help that none of us can give you."

Something inside Simon flared. Shot off like a rocket.

"You never tried to give me help. Not in Ohio. When you walked out on Mom. And definitely not here. The twins had Dr. Solomon, but besides Zachary, who did I ever have? You both work *all* the time. Late into the night even. And when you're not working, you're at town meetings, or with Realtors and potential buyers for this stupid property. Or therapy. Do either of you even care that I fell into an actual hole in the field this past week? It was deep. I had to pull myself up. I didn't tell anyone because I didn't want to scare you!"

Dad's eyes went wide. "I warned you about that field," he said quietly.

"But you still had no idea! It's like you don't even care!"

"If you really believe that, then all the better for us to look at the alternative."

Simon stood. He went to Bev and tried to take her hand. "*Please*. It's not fair."

Bev gave his fingers a squeeze, then pulled away. "Your father's right, Simon. We need to get you help."

CHAPTER TWENTY-SEVEN
ALEX

FROM HIS BEDROOM, Alex could hear the argument in the attic. He knew his sister must have been listening as well. He'd never heard Charlie sound so fed up. He understood that Simon had been forced out of Ohio for some kind of bad behavior the previous year, but could it have been worse than what he'd been up to lately? Writing stories on the walls in the basement? Inventing tales about Zachary as if he'd been living with them all this time?

Simon had been the one to point out the weird old door in the first place. Had this been his plan all along? To trick the twins into finding the Liars' Room? To make them all wonder who had really written those words? To make them question the strength of their relationships? If Simon had meant to wreck things for the family, he had pretty much gotten what he wanted. All they'd had since Dad died was their family, and now that seemed to be falling apart.

Sitting on his bed, Alex thought of Stella, just on the other side of the wall. He imagined that under different circumstances, they would have been together, holding hands, worrying about the shouting in the attic, but finding comfort in each other. Now, Stella was mad at him. And Alex was mad at Stella for taking Simon's side.

Still, he knocked on the wall over the head of his bedstead.

He waited for his sister to knock back.

Waited and waited.

In the morning, before the possibility of a breakfast together, the parents divided them up. Simon went with Charlie in his truck. Mom packed Alex and Stella into her Subaru.

"Where are we going?" Alex asked, fastening the safety belt in the back seat. Stella had taken shotgun.

"Errands. You two are going to be my assistants."

"What about Simon?" Stella asked. "Is Charlie taking him away to boarding school?"

Mom gave Stella a hard look. "Charlie has his own errands to run with Simon. And you weren't supposed to hear any of that."

"You all were pretty loud about it," Alex said.

Mom sighed. "I apologize. Charlie and Simon's mother have some more talking to do. It's none of our business."

Alex was confused. Wasn't Simon part of their family? Of course it was their business. "But — "

"*It's none of our business*," his mother repeated, turning the key in the ignition. She shook out her short hair. "Now, who's in the mood for bagels?"

After they stopped by the bagel shop on Main Street in Frost Meadow, they headed down the mountain. Mom had Stella navigate to a bunch of estate sales in the towns of Saugerties and Catskill before they crossed the river and made stops in Germantown, Red Hook, and Rhinebeck. After the fifth sale, Alex started to believe that Mom was not *actually* looking for antiques, or anything, really. They finished the day with a visit to a little bookstore café in an old stone building in Kingston where they all got chocolate chip cookies and cups of hot chocolate.

By the time evening rolled around and Charlie still hadn't returned to Wildwyck, Alex was certain that their parents' plan had been to keep the twins separated from Simon for the day. The trip had been an excuse to get them all out of the house — to get the house out of them. What Alex hadn't expected was for Stella to act as though they'd been separated too.

He hated that she'd half sided with Simon the previous day.

With one last strip of dusky orange light clinging to the horizon, he knocked on her door. She was reading a book. "You okay?" he asked. She finally glanced up.

She scoffed. "Not quite."

"You want to talk about it?" Alex felt like his words were footsteps through a minefield.

Stella exhaled. "I guess I'm just still sort of scared."

"Even though we've been turning on the lights?"

"I'm not sure that's helping anymore."

"I think it is." He dared to sit at the end of her mattress. Even though she scowled, he didn't get up. "What are you scared about?"

"I don't know." She crossed her arms. "*Everything.*"

Alex raised an eyebrow. "Could be a good title for something. *Scared of Everything.* Now, if only Mom would give us the phone back."

"I'm serious, Alex."

"*Scary Horse*," he went on. "I'll be sure to note that one for you."

Stella half smiled. "*Spooky Stallion* would be better."

"Come on," he said, grabbing the alarm clock off her nightstand. "We'll fix this."

"Fix it how?"

"You'll see."

Stella groaned, but she stood and followed him out of the room.

CHAPTER TWENTY-EIGHT
STELLA

OUTSIDE, THE AIR was biting. Alex led Stella across the courtyard to the driveway. Sconces by the front door poured a yellow glow across the grass. Alex held up the clock. Stella listened to the ticking of the second hand.

"Let's race," he said.

She'd been afraid this was what he was going to say. "I'm not sure — "

"Just one lap," Alex tried. "Around the house. See if you can beat your record. It'll make you feel better. I promise." It had been awhile since they'd played this game — not since Simon had disappeared around the far side of the barn a couple weeks back, on the day they'd come across the grave-yard in the woods. And before that, back in Brooklyn, when they'd go out in the evenings with Dad and race the block as fast as they could, only to come home out of breath and sweaty and then collapse onto the couch in a pile of giggles, three people deep.

Stella sighed. Maybe Alex was right. Maybe this would help, if only to make her remember the feeling of Dad running next to her, cheering her on. The three wings of the old school building were no bigger than that city block, she told herself. She got in her on-your-mark stance.

"As fast as you can. Get out of your head. Be wild. Okay?" Alex cleared his throat. "Ready? . . . Set . . . GO!"

Stella's sneaker slipped on a damp patch of ground, and she tore up a chunk of grass at the root. But then she found her footing, and before she knew it, she was at the end of the courtyard, heading around the edge of Wildwyck's darkened south wing, where Mom and Charlie had spent so much time working lately.

Coming to the next corner, Stella was surprised to find herself in sudden shadow. Here was the spot where the trees came closest to the building. She imagined the second hand ticking away on the alarm clock and pushed her way through the darkness.

Tick, tick, tick, tick.

Her feet landed in the same rhythm on the lawn.

But then she realized that the sound was not only in her mind. There were footfalls other than her own, and they were coming up quickly behind her.

Tick, tick, tick, tick.

"Alex?" Stella called over her shoulder, hoping he would answer, *Gotcha!* But there was no answer. She couldn't bring herself to slow down. "Simon?" she yelled louder. But had he and Charlie even come home yet?

She imagined herself riding on the muscled back of one of the horses she'd sketched in her notebook, a strong animal carrying her onward, away from danger. Sleek brown hair at her fingertips. Breath huffing as hooves clopped. Wind whipping against her face.

The footfalls were closer now. Only a few feet back.

Someone was after her. Breath sounded just behind her, raspy and ragged, like an animal. Not a horse. Something with shaggier fur. Sharper teeth.

This was no longer a race. This was a chase.

And if she slowed . . . if she stopped . . .

Stella felt a pain in her side.

She held her hand to her rib cage and steadied her breath.

No! Not a cramp! Not now!

Ahead was another corner, around which was the back door of their house. The yellow glow from the porch fell softly across the lawn. She just needed to break past the stitch. Reach the light.

Push a little harder. Go. GO.

She leapt up the bluestone steps and yanked at the door handle.

It was locked.

Tick. Tick. Tick. Tick.

She pulled again, but the door wouldn't budge. She turned and pressed her back against it. Looking around, she found that she was alone back here.

The sensation of being chased had been only that. A sensation.

She fought for steady breath.

Stella knocked at the door. She and Alex would have to finish this lap some other time. She couldn't believe she'd let him talk her into this, especially after what had happened yesterday. In the basement. In the dark. But that was the power of her twin. She tended to trust him, unquestioningly. And maybe that had been the problem. He'd never told her his entire plan for locking Simon in the stairwell. Could this still be part of it? Maybe it would never end. Peering through the window, she saw light down the hallway, but no one had heard her. Or maybe Mom had, but she was ignoring her. She banged again. Harder. Still no answer. Her knocking was so loud and strong, she was afraid she might break the glass.

Somewhere, a twig snapped.

Stella spun, looking to the shadowed trail from which the noise had come.

"Who's there?" Stella yelled, her voice strong and stable, unlike the feeling in her chest.

Was someone standing at the corner? Watching her? A dark silhouette, just beyond the reach of light? The person didn't answer. They only stared back. Her imagination became a flip-book, morphing from one possibility to another. As her eyes grew accustomed to the shadows, she could sense the person's size and shape. Tall. Taller than Alex or Simon. And broad. The edges of the form bleeding into the darkness behind it.

Was it Charlie? Why would he scare her like this?

Then, strangely, she wondered, if maybe it was Zachary . . . Or Gordon?

She thought of the box he had pulled from the dresser in the barn. Of the picture they'd found inside. *P. ~ 1975.* She thought of the figure Simon had said he'd seen moving through the woods near the graveyard, the girl, Peggy, and of the song that had flittered through her mind while she'd stood over her grave, growing faint.

This person didn't look like the girl from the Polaroid.

They looked like someone big enough and strong enough to hurt her.

She swallowed, scrounging for a kernel of courage to shout at the figure again. Scare him off. But the dryness in her throat fought back, and she couldn't find her breath. She gripped the doorknob harder, the edges of her vision growing dim.

The figure stepped closer. He dragged his hand along the outside wall. The house lights should have revealed his features. When he remained a blob of darkness, glitching and bleeding and blending with the surroundings, she realized that whoever, or whatever, she was looking at could not be a person.

Stella took off, continuing around the house, ignoring the lingering stitch, pretending that the path before her was perfectly clear. She pumped her arms. Her feet pounded against stony turf. The footsteps picked up again behind her. The ragged breathing too. Stella raced to the corner of the north wing, hugging it closely as she crossed to the front of the house. On this side, the fields stretched out toward the hillside, the bigger sky filled with stars providing a better view.

She imagined reaching arms, rattling bones, a widening jaw. "ALEX!" she called.

Where *was* he?

Grass crunched close behind her.

Tick, tick, tick, tick, tick.

Stella felt herself slowing. She couldn't outrun this thing. It would get her. Throw her to the ground. Wrap its fingers around her throat.

The breeze rustled her hair. A pressure filled her head.

She thought she could make out a growling sound, but maybe it was only her eardrums rattling.

Maybe all this was only in her mind.

One last corner. Up ahead. Her legs ached. There was a blade between her ribs, slicing into her diaphragm. Pain rippled down her back.

The thing was right there.

Right there.

And if she slowed even slightly —

Wham!

It felt like she'd crashed into a wall.

Falling to the grass, she rolled on her side. Something thumped the ground nearby. Through blurred sight, she focused on a light in the distance. Across the driveway.

She started to crawl.

There was no time . . . No time . . .

"Stella . . ." The voice came from a few feet away. It wheezed, trying to catch its breath, and she understood finally who she had run into. Alex had come looking for her. "What . . . happened?"

She sat up and peered back into the night, to the path from which she'd bolted. At the horizon, there lingered the slightest stretch of indigo. It was enough to show her that nothing was out there. The figure she'd seen, along with the footsteps and growling, had faded into the dark.

CHAPTER TWENTY-NINE
ALEX

WHEN THE SKY stopped spinning, Alex managed to crawl to his sister, who was sprawled out on the grass, staring off at the horizon. He touched her shoulder and she screamed, jolting away. But then she saw his face, and she leaned toward him and threw her arms around his neck.

She was sobbing. He squeezed her hard, as if he could shock her out of her tears, but she only held on more tightly. "Stella," he said, his voice still shaky from her crashing into him. "It's okay. I'm here."

After a few seconds, she caught her breath. Her eyes were wide and wild. Tears and snot were dripping from her chin. He couldn't remember the last time he'd seen her this upset. But then he did remember. It had been just after Mom had sat them down and told them —

"He w-was ch-chasing me," Stella sputtered.

"Who was chasing you?"

"Th-The *ghost*." Her jaw chattered. She was shivering now. He worried that she might have hit her head. His own shoulder ached where they'd collided.

"There is no ghost, Stella."

"I know what I saw! I saw . . ." She pointed toward the darkened north wing, toward the empty field. Alex waited for her to go on. But she deflated — the energy that had brought her so ferociously back around to the courtyard was ebbing away. He stood and held out his hand. "Come on. Let's get back inside."

"But I don't want Mom and Charlie to see — "

"They won't," he promised. "This is just you and me. You and me. Okay?"

When she rose, she looked into his eyes and seemed to find herself again. "Okay," she whispered.

Upstairs, he cleaned her face with a washcloth in the bathroom sink. Then he brought her to her room with a glass of water and a box of tissues. Together they sat on her bed again. He asked her what she'd seen, and she told him.

"You really think it was a ghost," Alex stated. Stella nodded firmly. "There's no other explanation for what happened out there?" He hesitated. "Because, sometimes, when I run too fast, I feel faint. I see splotches of shadow. My head pounds. The world seems like it could . . . melt away." Stella sighed, seeing where he was going. "Hold up. I made a mistake. Okay? I shouldn't have suggested the lap. Not this late in the day. And especially not after you'd already told me you were feeling scared. This was my fault. I'm sorry."

Stella stared down at her quilt. "You say that . . . but are you really?"

"Yes, of course!"

"I was fine in here until you insisted I follow you outside."

"I was trying to help you."

"You were trying to do *something*. Exactly what, I'm not sure."

Alex pressed his lips together. "You still think I wrote that stuff in the basement. To get Simon in trouble."

"What I think is that . . ." She looked up again, hurt making her eyes look glossy. "I want to read my book."

Charlie and Simon arrived home shortly after that.

Alex, Stella, and Simon spent that night separately in their rooms — unplugged from all tech, because now they were grounded even harder — while Charlie and Mom listened to political candidates debating loudly on the television in the den below. Alex woke the next morning feeling anxious. What he and Stella had been through with Simon over the weekend could have bonded them, but the opposite had happened. Whoever had written those words on the basement walls was getting exactly what they'd wanted. Alex knew he'd have to try harder, to keep them from winning.

His gut had long told him to not trust his stepbrother, but now his brain was telling him to not trust his gut. Life is weird when even parts of your body can lie to you.

Maybe he didn't have to full-on *believe* in ghosts. But maybe, just maybe, he could give both Stella and Simon the benefit of the doubt. It wouldn't make things worse than they already were, and if nothing else, maybe the two of them might stop looking at Alex like *he'd* been the cause of their latest problems.

So, when the three climbed aboard the long yellow bus at the end of the driveway the next morning, Alex waved for Stella and Simon to follow him to the back row.

He took the window seat. Stella sat beside him.

Simon perched across the aisle. "So, what, we're *friends* now?"

"I wouldn't go that far," Alex said. "But we're closer." He felt himself blush. "Closer to an answer, I mean."

"So you finally think Wildwyck is haunted?" Stella asked.

"I don't know. I mean, I know what I saw and what I heard. And I think . . . at this point . . . I'm willing to believe that none of us made that happen."

"That's a start," Simon said.

"But we need to do more," Alex said. "I don't know about you two, but I don't want another experience like Saturday ever again."

"Do more *what*?" Stella asked.

"Investigating," Alex answered. Both Stella and Simon sighed, glancing at each other unsurely. Alex had to use all his energy to keep from exploding at them. He thought of Dr. Solomon's technique and managed to scrub away the pressure building in his skull. "Together."

CHAPTER THIRTY
ALEX

ALEX SEARCHED FOR Gordon before classes started. He'd wanted to tell him everything that had happened over the weekend, to see if Gordon had any ideas, or if he knew of any other stories about Wildwyck that could point them toward an answer. But Gordon was nowhere to be found.

There was someone else Alex knew who might be able to help.

At lunch, he convinced Stella to return to his math teacher's classroom. They knocked. Mr. Levinthal waved them forward, wearing a look that said: *Haven't we already done this?*

To Alex's surprise, Stella spoke first. "Mr. Levinthal, we need your help." Maybe the scare from the previous night had shocked her into bravery.

"That's great, because I love to help," Mr. Levinthal answered. "But the amount of help I give usually depends on what kind of help one needs." He raised an eyebrow and waited for one of them to go on.

"Strange things have been happening at Wildwyck," Stella said.

Alex felt his face heat up. This was not how he would have begun. Mr. Levinthal had gotten spooked last time. They must be careful now.

"Really," said the teacher. "Strange in what way?"

Alex knew it would be best to leave out the ghostly parts of the story. But that's why they were here, wasn't it? To see if he knew anything more about them? "We found some writing on the walls in the basement."

Mr. Levinthal set his jaw. "What did it say?"

"It was . . . a kind of journal."

Stella interrupted. "Mr. Levinthal, what do you know about the punishment rooms at Wildwyck?"

Mr. Levinthal gave a sort of scoff and then looked to the ceiling before closing his eyes. "You've heard those stories," he said quietly, almost to himself. He obviously didn't want to talk about this. He opened his mouth, his tongue making a soft clicking sound, then inhaled sharply. "All I'll say about that is I struggled with the headmaster's . . . ideas for discipline. They're the main reason I left that place."

"Did Peggy Wildwyck have anything to do with those rooms?" Alex asked. He figured it was better than, *Is Peggy Wildwyck haunting the old school?*

Mr. Levinthal pondered the lines in his palms for several seconds. "Not that I know of. She was the headmaster's daughter. Lived with her parents in the main building, but she went to school here in the village."

"What happened to her?" Stella asked. She was clutching the Polaroid of Peggy suddenly, as if she'd produced it magically. Alex was surprised that she was still holding on to it. She placed it on Mr. Levinthal's desk, turned so that Peggy was peering up at him with glinting eyes.

Mr. Levinthal looked more and more uncomfortable.

Alex worried this was all too close to what had ended their last conversation, when Stella had brought up Peggy dying.

This time, however, the teacher picked up the picture and went on. "I remember feeling like . . . it was almost . . . my fault."

"Your fault?" Stella asked. "How?"

Mr. Levinthal spoke as if the photograph had somehow hypnotized him. As if the twins weren't there anymore. "I was the one who found them in the barn that night. I'd been walking back to the cottages from the main building when I saw a light up the hill. It was raining hard. Still, I knew that no one should have been in there. Not that late. Not in the dark. When I opened the door, I saw her sitting on the floor across from a boy — one of the Wildwyck students. I didn't know him well. A small candle was lit atop a blanket laid out between them. They were both soaking wet from the rain and too wrapped up in their conversation to notice me. I remember . . . she held his hand, as if to comfort him.

"I knocked. They were surprised to see me. I wasn't angry or shocked. I told them simply that it was time to head back inside. The boy wrapped Peggy in the blanket. I brought them to the main building, to the headmaster's apartments. I left them there for her parents, Hart and Ada, to deal with. I knew . . . I *knew* there'd be consequences. But still . . . I left them."

He picked up the photograph and then glanced at the twins again. "She got sick after that. She'd had some long-term health issues. But Hart and Ada said it was from being out in the rain that night." Mr. Levinthal handed the photo back to Stella. "When she passed, the whole school was in shock."

Alex flinched. He knew that Peggy had gotten sick, but hearing how quickly it had happened . . . He felt a deep cold.

"The students. The staff. The teachers. No one could believe it. She was so young. *So* young." He pressed his fingers against the desk and tented his palms just above them. "You cannot take your lives for granted."

"We don't," Alex whispered. His father's face flashed in his mind.

"I left because I didn't agree with how the Wildwycks punished that boy, the one in the barn that night. He'd stood firm that they had just been talking. That they were good friends. But the Wildwycks insisted he wasn't telling the truth." Mr. Levinthal exhaled slowly. "They said those rooms were *special places*. Spaces where students were . . . *corrected*. The Temper Room was padded with cushions to keep angry students from 'hurting themselves and others.' In the Cheaters' Room, students were supposed to write on chalkboards until 'they got it right.' And the Liars' Room. That one was painted black. No lights. No sound. 'A place where a student was unable to contemplate the falsities of the world . . . Where all that remained was the truth,' as Hart Wildwyck once told me. I'll never forget it."

"That's horrible," said Alex. His stomach shifted, making him queasy. Stella held her hand to her mouth.

"Hart and Ada put the boy in that dark room. Kept him there." The man shuddered. "I couldn't teach in a place that would treat a child like that . . . So I left. I stayed with my parents in Hedston while looking for another job. And when I found one, I never looked back."

"What happened to the boy?" Alex asked. "The boy in the Liars' Room?"

Mr. Levinthal glanced at the clock on the wall over the door. "I didn't keep in touch with anyone from Wildwyck, so I'm not one hundred percent sure. But I believe that when he got out, the boy didn't stick around either. Last I heard, he'd run off. Disappeared."

"Do you remember his name?" Stella asked.

Mr. Levinthal nodded. He looked exhausted, as if he'd just sprinted around the whole school. "His name was Joshua. Joshua Hendrix."

CHAPTER THIRTY-ONE
STELLA

"TODAY WAS WILD," said Alex, taking a seat in the bus's last row. "I did not expect Mr. Levinthal to just spill all that."

Stella felt annoyed he was talking as if everything were fine again between them. "Me neither," she answered, looking around for Simon. He must have been dawdling with his friends in the fifth grade hallway.

"So, what do we know now that we didn't know before?" Alex asked. "Want to write it down so we don't forget?"

Stella grabbed a pen from her bag and then turned to a blank page in her sketchbook. "Mr. L found Peggy in the barn with a kid named Joshua Hendrix. Her parents blamed Joshua for what happened to her. And they locked him in the Liars' Room."

"Which Mr. L didn't agree with. So he quit."

"Right . . ." Stella had a thought. She reached into her bag and retrieved Peggy's water-damaged journal.

Alex sniffed. "I didn't know you've been carrying that thing around."

"Maybe there's *lots* you don't know about me," she answered, satisfied to see the surprised look on his face. Flipping through to the pages that still had legible writing, she copied the words she could make out into her sketchbook.

"New friend, J . . ."

"A special connection . . ."
"Mom and Dad won't let . . ."
"Needs help . . ."
"a's family is gone . . ."
"We're meeting up again tonight. He says he has lots to tell me . . ."

"The new friend is obviously Joshua," she said. "Maybe Peggy felt like they had a special connection."

"Makes sense," Alex said, not looking at her. Stella had obviously hurt him, and she wasn't sure how to feel about it. "Peggy lived at Wildwyck. She must have known some of the students."

"But her mom and dad weren't happy about it? They didn't want her talking to the boys?" Stella considered Peggy's writing. *"a's family is gone,"* Stella read again. "She could have meant Joshua's family. His name ends with an *a*. Mr. L said that when he found them they were holding hands. He had lots to tell her? Maybe . . . Joshua felt like Peggy was his family. Like a brother."

"What are you two going on about?" Simon stood in the aisle, watching them.

Stella started, "We were just talking — "

"About my math teacher," Alex interrupted.

Stella rolled her eyes. "We spoke with Mr. Levinthal again today." Alex clenched his fists. She shrugged at him. Did he want them all to work together, like he'd said that morning, or not? She went on, telling Simon what Alex's teacher had said.

Simon sat in the seat across from them. "Those are the names from the writing in the basement. Joshua and Peggy."

Stella glanced at Alex, shocked. How had they not put that together? "That's it, then," Simon added, his face lighting up. "This kid. Joshua? He's gotta be our ghost!"

Alex shook his head. "I'm not saying I believe in ghosts just yet, but Mr. Levinthal did say that he heard after the Wildwycks let him out of the Liars' Room, he took off. So how could Joshua even *be* a ghost at our house? He left."

"Well . . . Maybe Mr. Levinthal is hiding something," Simon said.

"You think he could be lying?" Stella asked.

"Maybe Mr. Levinthal is the one who snuck into the north wing and wrote on the walls."

Stella smiled. "Yeah. Right. And he's going to show up next time Mom and Charlie are out, and he'll make sure that you, me, and Alex never tell anyone what we suspect."

"*I* don't suspect that!" Alex spat.

"A murderous math teacher?" Simon chuckled. "Stranger things have happened."

Stella was quiet for a moment. "If it *is* a ghost . . . what do we do?"

"If there's one thing I know about ghosts, it's that they tend to scare people," Simon said.

"What if it wants something from us?" Stella asked.

"Like?"

"What if it *is* Peggy? Maybe she wants us to . . . I don't know what."

"We already know it's not Peggy," Alex said. "Whoever is doing this seems . . . angry. *So* not like the girl in that Polaroid."

"Oh, so *now* you believe?" Simon asked.

"That's not what I said."

"Would you two please just stop. You're giving me a headache." The boys glanced at each other, impressed. The bus engine rumbled awake. The driver closed the door and shifted into gear. Stella looked out the window. "All day, I've been thinking about the boy who was locked up in the Liars' Room," she went on. "If there *is* a seed of truth inside every lie, maybe the writing in the basement isn't Zachary's story. Maybe it's *Joshua's*. The shoplifting. Getting in trouble. Not being believed. All those things could be why he was sent to Wildwyck in the first place."

"You don't think that Joshua was a bad person?" Simon asked. "Even after everything that's happened to us at Wildwyck."

Stella made a sour face, then shook her head. "We did some of those things ourselves. Does that mean *we're* bad people?"

"Maybe some of us are," Alex whispered, as if to himself. He must have known they'd hear. Stella glared at him, then looked over to Simon, who gave her a sad smile.

She glared at him too.

Back home, the boys ran upstairs to their rooms to do who knew what.

Mom was in the kitchen, rummaging through the cupboards. Stella stood in the doorway, watching. When Mom turned, she jumped and dropped a pot. It clattered to the floor along with several lids.

"Sorry!" Stella rushed to help pick them up.

"Look at me," Mom said, "jumping at shadows."

"I'm not a shadow," Stella answered. "I'm your daughter."

Mom laughed. "Thank goodness for that." She took the pot and the lids and set them on the counter. "I'm thinking it's a nice evening for homemade chicken soup."

"Simon's going to be mad. He hates soup."

"Good thing there are four other people in this house who love it. Want to help?"

Stella couldn't think of anything she would rather do.

Minutes later, she was at the cutting board, peeling carrots. The skins were flying all over the counter. Mom was doing something at the table with the uncooked chicken. Stella didn't like looking at raw meat, so she spoke over her shoulder, "Mom, how much did you know about this place when you and Charlie bought it?"

"A little bit. It's an old house. There's so much history. We're still learning."

"Did Alex tell you his math teacher used to teach at Wildwyck?"

"I think so? Maybe?"

"We were talking with him about it today." Stella's stomach ached. She knew Alex wouldn't want her to share this with their mother. Not yet. But she knew it was the right thing to do. "He told us some scary things."

"That's not cool," said Mom.

"No, but, I mean, we asked him to tell us."

"That's not cool either, Stella!"

"Mom, just . . . listen. Please?" Stella started from the

beginning. She told her mother about Peggy and Joshua and the Liars' Room and why Mr. Levinthal had quit teaching there. When she was done, she turned from the sink to find her mother leaning against the table, watching her.

"That's a lot, honey."

"I know, and it's weird, right? Like, maybe some of the ghost stories Simon told us are . . . true." She wanted to tell her what had happened the night before, being chased around the house by that shadow figure. But she'd done so much hard work with Dr. Solomon over the years, she didn't want Mom to think she was moving backward.

"You know that Charlie and I are doing everything we can to keep you kids safe, right?"

Stella forced a laugh. "Yeah. Sure. I know that."

"Good," Mom said, turning back to the chicken. "We'd never let anything hurt you. Not even a ghost."

Stella raced over and hugged her. Mom squeaked with surprise. "What's this for?" she asked, squeezing her back.

"I appreciate you," Stella answered. She kept the real reason to herself. She thought it was incredibly sad that her mother imagined she could keep any of them safe for much longer. Stella knew there was so much bad out there in the world, waiting for them. Cruel people in power. Like headmasters with strange ideas about punishment.

Or sickness.

Or taxicabs that fly through city intersections without pausing to look for pedestrians.

CHAPTER THIRTY-TWO
ALEX

ON TUESDAY, THE bus pulled up in front of the school twenty minutes before the first bell was set to ring. This gave Alex, Stella, and Simon time to head to the library and log on to one of the computers. Charlie had restricted their access at home completely. Just as Alex was typing the name into the search field, he felt a tapping on his shoulder. He spun to find Gordon Weinberger grinning down at them.

"It's nice to see you three together for once," Gordon said. "What's up?"

Alex wasn't sure he wanted Gordon to know. Suddenly, it all felt personal and a little bit tender. Before he could deny anything, Simon spoke up. "We're researching our ghost."

Alex tensed. "Well, not really —"

Gordon's face lit up. "Ooh, count me in!" He pulled up a chair and sat down. Peering at the screen, he read what Alex had written. "Joshua H?"

"Hendrix," said Stella, scooting closer. She told him what they'd learned from Mr. Levinthal.

"And you think he's the one haunting the place?"

Alex tried to answer, "At this point, we can't really say —"

"We have *so much* to tell you," Simon interrupted, his eyes bulging.

Alex had to hold back from snapping at him.

"Yeah? Like what?" Gordon asked.

Simon spent the next few minutes filling in Gordon on what had happened over the weekend. Gordon sat, rapt. Alex couldn't help but think that their time would be better spent looking up Joshua Hendrix's name. But then he figured it might be good to have another team member. Gordon had been the one to find the metal box in the barn, after all.

Simon had barely finished telling the details of the writing they'd uncovered in the basement when the bell sounded.

"You can't leave it like that!" Gordon shivered. "What happened next? Who wrote all that stuff on the walls?"

"That's what we're trying to figure out," said Simon.

Alex looked hard into Gordon's face, trying to see what was behind his enthusiasm. Did Gordon know more about the writing than he was letting on?

That was the thing about being manipulated over and over. After a while, it was hard to trust *anyone*.

"We should get going or we'll be late," Stella said.

Gordon lowered his voice. "Can you all meet me back here after fourth period? I'll sneak out of my classroom."

Stella and Simon nodded.

Alex took a deep breath. "I'll try to make it happen."

He blinked and the first four periods were gone.

As Alex made his way back to the library, bathroom pass in hand, he felt his skin grow clammy. His nerves were getting to him. Flashes of being trapped in the room in the basement kept blinking in his brain.

He saw Stella sitting with Simon and Gordon at a table at the far side of the room near the windows. They were huddled over a mess of papers. He snuck past the front desk, where the librarian was eating lunch with her assistant. "What's all this?" he whispered.

"I used the computer in my classroom," said Gordon. "I couldn't find anything about Joshua. But I did locate an article in the archives of the local paper about Peggy Wildwyck's memorial service."

Not what we need, really, Alex thought, reaching for the pages. *But, at least it's something.* He scanned the article. After the particulars of where and when the memorial took place, it mentioned Peggy's brief, tragic illness. There were quotes from her parents and her teachers, talking about how smart and kindhearted she'd been. How she'd never judged anyone. How she participated in many community activities and programs.

"Look here," said Simon, kneeling on his chair and pointing to one particular spot. "Does this sound familiar?"

Alex noticed the name printed just above Simon's fingernail. He read the line aloud: *"'Peggy was a truly remarkable girl,' said Wildwyck student Ship Curtis. 'I'll miss her more than words can say. And I know my classmates feel the same. We plan on doing a fundraiser in her honor. She'll never be forgotten. Not while our school stands.'"*

"Curtis?" said Stella. "Why does that name sound familiar?

"Your mom told us about him," Simon said. "Doesn't Mr. Curtis own the bookstore in town?"

"That's right!"

"He must have had a crush on her," Alex said. "A fund-raiser? *She'll never be forgotten?*"

"Oh, he is *definitely* hiding something," Gordon added.

"You think so?" Simon asked.

"Should we go see him?" Gordon said. "Confront him? Make him tell us all about it?"

"We can't cut class," Alex said.

"We'll call him," Stella said. "Call his store and . . . do what Gordon said."

Alex shook his head. "We don't have a phone."

"I can get a phone," said Gordon.

"You have a phone?" Simon asked, excited.

"I can *get* one." Gordon glanced at the checkout desk. "But you all need to hide. Just for a minute or two."

Wide-eyed, Stella asked, "What are you going to do?"

"It's better if you don't ask," he answered with a grin, his voice just barely a whisper.

Alex followed his sister and stepbrother into an aisle between bookshelves, just out of the librarian's view. None of them knew what to say. This was not how they had expected their research to go.

Seconds later, Gordon sauntered back around the corner of the bookshelf wearing a satisfied smile. He held up a phone, waving it.

"Whose is that?" Alex asked.

"Ms. Mitchell's." The librarian. "She's good friends with my grandmother. I said I needed to call home, so she let me borrow it."

Stella shifted her weight. "But we're not allowed to have phones during school hours. That's . . . weird."

"Weird, yes, but now we've got a phone! And it's unlocked." Gordon opened the browser and looked up the number for Ship Curtis's bookstore. He touched the call button, and the line connected.

A muffled voice sounded. "Our Book Shop. How can I help you?"

Gordon held the phone to his ear. "Mr. Curtis?"

He kept the phone off-speaker, so the librarian wouldn't hear them. Alex knew it was for the best, but he wished he could hear the man's response.

"Yeah, hi," Gordon went on, making excited eye contact with Alex. "This is Alex Hill."

Alex flinched. *What was he doing?*

"My mom came into your store a couple weeks ago? . . . That's right. *Wildwyck*."

Alex looked to Stella and Simon. They appeared to be just as confused as he was.

"Anyway, our family has been having a pretty strange week up at your old school. I was wondering if I could ask you a couple questions?" The muffled voice sounded, but now the words were merely noise. "Really? That's so nice of you." Gordon nodded at them, then added, "The thing is, I'd like to know what you did to Joshua Hendrix?"

Alex felt weak. He grabbed at the nearest bookshelf to steady himself.

"I'm pretty sure he didn't run away from the school . . . No, I'm almost positive about that . . . Proof? How about his spirit haunting Wildwyck? . . . No, I'm not joking . . . Did *you* kill him, or was it someone else?"

"Gordon!" Stella blurted out in a harsh whisper.

Simon's face was a mask of amazement.

Alex swiped at the phone, but Gordon stepped past him, away from the group, farther down the aisle. Gordon raised his palm to keep them at bay, looking determined. "Then who did?" Puzzled, he added, "Mr. Curtis?" He glanced at the phone, then held it up so the others could see. "He hung up."

Alex couldn't hold back. "What is *wrong* with you?"

"That was *bad*," Stella said. "That was really bad, Gordon. We were already worried about him. Now you made him angry."

"Yeah, at *me*!" Alex added.

"Keep your voices down," Gordon whispered. "I didn't tell Ms. Mitchell I was with you all back here."

"But what did he say?" Simon asked.

"What do you think he said?" Alex said harshly. "*Yes, I murdered Joshua Hendrix? Yes, it's his ghost who wrote on the walls in your basement, pretending to be Simon's brother, saying a bunch of horrible things about your family, so that you'd all end up hating each other?*"

Simon turned to Gordon. "*Did* he say that?"

"Of course not!" Alex said, almost feeling the need to laugh. "The guy hung up!"

"What if he calls Mom?" Stella asked. "What if he tells her what *you* said?" She glanced at Gordon, who didn't look the slightest bit sorry. "We're so dead."

Alex reached for the phone. "Give me that." He was

surprised when Gordon handed it over. He opened the recent calls screen. "I'm pretty sure he doesn't have Mom's cell number. And Charlie has been working on the landline." He pulled up the bookstore's number, then blocked it and deleted the record of the call. "And now he won't be able to call *this* phone back." He sighed and handed the phone to Gordon again. "Don't you understand how serious this is? It's not just a fun story. It's not just a local legend. The things that have been happening at Wildwyck are real. And they're scary." Gordon licked his lips, finally looking like he understood Alex's outrage. "Why did you do that?"

"I was trying to help. Depending on how Mr. Curtis responds, we might just find out the rest of what he . . ." Gordon stopped short. His eyes went wide as he peered behind them.

A shadow fell across the aisle.

Alex turned to find Ms. Mitchell glaring at them.

CHAPTER THIRTY-THREE
STELLA

"WHAT ARE YOU doing back here?" asked the librarian.

Stella felt herself go stiff. Something clunked to the floor beside her. Turning, she saw Gordon disappear around the far corner. He'd just run off? *Coward*.

"Is that my phone?"

Stella glanced down. The phone was facing downward, lying near the heel of her sneaker. The protective cover was decorated with black and white cats that fit together in a puzzling pattern. Stella picked it up and handed it over.

"How'd you get this? It was in my pocket just a few minutes ago."

Simon spoke up. "Gordon said he asked you to borrow it."

Ms. Mitchell frowned at Alex. "Why would you say that?"

"No, I'm Alex," Alex said. "Gordon Weinberger. He was *just . . .*" He glanced around the library as if looking for the boy. "He took off when he saw you. He said you're friends with his grandmother and that you let him borrow it. Please, don't call our parents."

Ms. Mitchell sucked at her teeth. Her look of surprise fell away, replaced by what, Stella wasn't sure. The woman motioned for them to sit at a nearby table. "You're Simon and Stella and Alex." She said it like a question she already knew the answer to. "New to Frost Meadow Middle."

Stella looked around for Gordon again, but he must have already slipped out of the library. She swallowed and nodded.

"Look, I know things have been . . . *tough* for you kids the past few years. And moving to a new town and making new friends can feel pretty intense. But this?" She held up her phone. "*This* is not okay."

Simon tried, "We swear — "

"Please, don't swear. Not in my library." Ms. Mitchell smiled. "I want all our students to feel like this is a safe space. But it has to feel like a safe space for *me* too. And that cannot happen if you take things that do not belong to you." Stella could see Simon about to argue again, so she grabbed his wrist and squeezed. "Tell you what . . . You promise to come in and help reshelve some books sometime this week, and I promise I won't mention what happened here to anyone. Deal?"

Stella couldn't believe their luck. She also couldn't believe how badly she wanted to tell off Gordon Weinberger.

After the last bell, she looked all over the school for him, but apparently he did not want to be found. She barely made it onto the bus before the doors closed. She found her brother and Simon in the same seats as they'd been that morning. She plopped herself down beside them and said, "Well, *that* didn't go as planned."

"Doesn't feel like anything does anymore," Alex answered.

Stella expected them all to go off on Gordon, but when the boys said nothing else, she realized that there was nothing else to say. The kid was a jerk. As much of a jerk as the rest of the kids at their school. Maybe more so because he'd kept his jerkiness hidden from them until they felt like they were all friends.

At least there were the *Ms. Mitchells* of the world.

As the three rode the rest of the way in silence, Stella took out her sketchbook. She examined the floor plans she'd copied over a week ago, remembering where they'd led her. She thought again of the darkness of that awful room. She imagined what it must have felt like for Joshua Hendrix to be locked in there for days and days. She turned to a blank page and started doodling another unicorn idea for her bedroom mural, which she promised herself she would paint soon.

Walking up the driveway from the bus stop, Stella felt herself flood with a sudden fear. Was it from Gordon's betrayal? Was she scared of how her mother might respond when they walked into the house? Was it the house itself? She glanced at Alex, who was staring at the pebble-strewn ground. Simon was hurrying on ahead of them. Were they all okay now, despite the lies they'd read on the basement walls? Would the family recover? Or was another surprise just around the corner? Maybe it would be best to stop investigating the house and its former residents. It had only led to more fear, more tension, more trouble. Maybe it would be easier to sleep at night if they turned all the lights *off* instead. She wanted to mention it to Alex, but he still looked angry. About the day. About the week. About Simon. About Dad. Like the rest of the mysteries that were swirling around her, like the colorful fallen leaves along the path, it might be best to sweep them aside and just keep walking.

By the time they made it across the courtyard to the

front door, Stella's anxiety was rippling through her body. But when Mom called out from the den — "Hey, all! How was school?" — Stella felt at least 50 percent better. Alex disappeared down the hall. Stella overheard him answer that it had been fine.

Ms. Mitchell and Mr. Curtis hadn't reached out after all.

Stella didn't want to be around the boys, didn't want to talk about any next steps. She raced up the staircase to her room and closed the door. Then she laid on her bed and opened *The Secret Garden* by Frances Hodgson Burnett, which she'd been trying to read since the start of school.

It was just past dark when there was a rapping at her door. Stella sat up with a gasp. A dream of crumbling mansions lingered. Dark hallways. Echoes crying out from behind locked doors. Endless wilderness where it was easy to get lost.

"Stella?" She watched the doorknob twist and turn. "Stella, let me in!"

The world of the dream crumbled and she leapt out of bed. She found Alex standing in the hall, bug-eyed and panting. He pushed past her into the room. "Hey!" she cried out. But he turned and held his finger to his lips. He switched off the light on her bedside table, then waved her over to the window. "What are you — "

"Someone's here," her brother interrupted. "Look."

Stella sighed and stomped over to where Alex was crouched, peering just over the windowsill. He pulled her down beside him. Outside, a car had parked in front of the long shed. Two headlights shone brightly, lighting up the courtyard. "It's Charlie," she said. "Coming home from wher-ever he spent the afternoon."

"That's a sedan. Not a pickup truck."

"Okay. So?"

Alex spun on her, his jaw askew, as if he couldn't believe she'd ask such a thing. "Do you not remember what happened this afternoon? When *I* called up a complete stranger and accused him of *murder*?"

It all came rushing back, along with a full-body pinprick sensation of dread. Very much like when the shadowy figure had chased her around the perimeter of the house.

Across the yard, the headlights blinked off. The driver's door opened. Someone stepped out.

CHAPTER THIRTY-FOUR
STELLA

"WHAT ARE YOU two doing?"

Stella dropped away from the window and turned to the door. Simon was staring at them curiously.

"Get down!" Alex whispered.

Startled, Simon brought himself to a squat. "Who's out there?" he asked.

"Who do you think?"

"Are you two really *that* scared of my dad?"

"It's not your dad," said Stella. "We think it's the owner of the book shop."

"Oh," Simon said. "Yeah. That's really bad. But, I mean, can't we explain what Gordon did? That it wasn't our fault?"

Alex pressed his lips and nodded curtly. "We can explain all we want . . . That is, if he gives us a chance."

"He wouldn't hurt us," Simon insisted, sounding as if he was trying to convince himself.

"How would *you* respond to someone who accused you of killing one of your friends forty years ago?"

"If I didn't do it, I wouldn't respond at all."

"And if you *did* do it?"

Simon crawled across the room to them.

Alex peered over the window ledge. "He's gone!"

Stella checked too. The courtyard was empty. That was when they heard a pounding at the front door below.

Bang, bang, bang!

"I'm coming!" Mom called out from the first floor.

Stella scrambled out to the hallway. "Mom, wait!" she shouted. But then she heard the latch click and the hinges squeak, and she knew it was too late. The three ran to the landing and grabbed at the banister. Looking down, Stella saw a man following their mother through the foyer toward the kitchen doorway.

"What does he want?" Alex whispered.

"I didn't hear."

Just before he passed into the kitchen, the man looked up at them. His eyes were dark, his brow lowered.

There was the sound of chairs scraping against the floor. Mom was offering him a seat. "Can I get you something to drink?" she asked.

"Water would be great."

Stella edged past her brother and slowly made her way down the staircase. She stopped before the kitchen entry, holding out her arm to keep the boys back. She listened to the fridge open and shut, the sound of ice plopping into tall glasses of water, the glasses sliding across the table.

"It's nice to see you again, Ship. What brings you out?"

Mr. Curtis.

Stella grabbed at the ends of her hair and yanked down.

"I wanted to talk, but I couldn't find your number," Mr. Curtis said. "If your kids would all just come out from around the corner . . ."

A chair scraped. Stella froze. Footsteps padded across tile. Mom came through the door and let out a yelp. "You scared me!" she said. "What are you all doing down here?"

Stella wanted to take her mother's hand and pull her out the front door. She pressed her lips together and made her eyes wide, nodding toward the kitchen to signal that something was wrong.

But then Simon blurted out, "He said he wanted to talk to us," and Mom ignored Stella's warning.

Instead, she sighed and waved for them to follow her into the kitchen. "I'm so sorry, Mr. Curtis. My children have been struggling with manners lately." She shot them all a fierce look.

Mr. Curtis stood. He wore a blue, plaid, button-down shirt, khaki pants, and brown leather boots. A small belly bulged over his belt. Short, black, curly hair wrapped around the sides of his head, leaving the top slightly fuzzy and mostly bald. His skin was dark and his eyes were soft. He didn't look like a murderer, but still Stella cowered. "I'm not sure if you're aware, Mrs. Hill, but I received a call this afternoon from someone claiming to be Alex." Mom pierced Alex with a death-ray glare. "At first I thought it was a prank . . . He said some pretty awful things."

"It wasn't me!" Alex tried.

But Mr. Curtis held up his hand.

"I haven't been able to stop thinking about the call all day."

"What did my son say?" Mom asked.

"He wanted to know what had happened to a former

Wildwyck student. One of my classmates when I was in attendance. A long time ago, the headmaster, Hart, and his wife, Ada, kept a boy named Joshua Hendrix sequestered in a place here at Wildwyck we used to call the Liars' Room."

Mom shook her head. "I don't understand. Joshua? He was . . . *real*?" She knew the name from the writing they'd discovered in the basement. Joshua: the fake-Zachary's supposed friend. Charlie had taken photos of the writing, and Mom must have read all of it. The stories. The lies.

"He was real." Mr. Curtis shook his head. "And for some reason, today, Alex accused me of hurting him." He glanced at Stella and the boys. "I came here to make it clear that I had nothing whatsoever to do with Joshua. The truth of what happened to him was something I thought I'd put out of my head decades ago." He gripped at his hands, motioning as if washing them clean. He looked to the kids. "Since Alex's call, his accusation, things have been coming back to me. It's still a bit of a jumble, but I thought it would be best to just . . . get all this off my chest." He stared at Alex. "If memory is a liar, then hurt is its teacher, whispering instructions on how to lie *better*."

"I'm sorry, Mr. Curtis," Mom interrupted. "Maybe we should do this some other time, when my husband is home." Her eyes went wide, as if realizing her mistake. "He's due back any second, but still, I'm not sure that — "

Mr. Curtis held on to the back of his chair. "I don't mean to scare you. I should've looked harder for your phone number. Please. If you'd just hear me out . . . You and the kids . . . I think . . . I think we'll all . . ." He closed his eyes. "Shortly after the death of their daughter, the Wildwycks locked Joshua in the Liars' Room. Claimed that he'd been lying about his friendship with her. Kept him there for days.

"We boys were sick about it. We knew Peggy's parents were mad she was gone and were taking it out on Joshua. Taking it out on *all* of us, in a way. Some of the boys wanted to open that door. But then none of us wished to be locked in with him if we were caught. And we were always caught." Mr. Curtis shuddered. "After a while, we could hear him shouting. Pounding on the walls. Calling for help."

Simon huddled close to Stella. Alex looked to the two of them and squinted.

"Joshua must have been terrified, locked away in total darkness," Mr. Curtis continued. "The best us boys could do was creep to the door and slip messages underneath, so that he'd know he wasn't alone. Pictures of Peggy. Scraps of paper, telling him to stay strong. That we were all there for him. Most likely, he wouldn't have been able to read or see any of it. But we had to do *something.*

"One night, a storm came through. I'm not sure if your family has been in town long enough to experience a mountain squall, but they can be bad. The school lost power. There was trouble out at the teachers' cottages; a piece of roof had been ripped off. And the barn was hit hard. The storm . . . It tore up everything."

Stella tried to listen, but the sound of the wind outside was fighting for her attention.

"Did you know that this building used to be surrounded by giant oak trees? I say *used to* because that night, many of them fell. During the worst of it, I thought I heard Joshua crying. One of the biggest of them crashed down, right onto the school." Mr. Curtis swallowed hard. "After that, the crying stopped."

Goose bumps tightened Stella's skin.

A gust rocked the old building, whipping through the eaves. Briefly, it sounded like someone shouting, far away.

Mom shook her head. "The boy died? Here. In this building?"

Mr. Curtis nodded. "Up in the attic. In the Liars' Room."

Stella spoke up. "But I thought . . ." She glanced at her brothers. "Isn't the Liars' Room down in the basement? That's where we found — "

"The Cheaters' Room was in the basement," Mr. Curtis said. "The walls down there were covered in chalkboards, so the boys could write out the lessons that they'd been caught cheating on." He inhaled quickly. "No. The *Liars'* Room . . . That was up in the attic."

"In my bedroom?" Simon asked, the color draining from his face.

"I'm sure that's not true," Mom said, coming to Simon's side.

"Oh, it's true," Mr. Curtis replied. "You kids wanted to know so badly what I did to our friend Joshua." He wiped at his mouth. "I could have saved him. Any of us could have. But we didn't. We were too scared."

The wind was howling now. Wailing. The walls rattled, and the lights flickered. Suddenly, Stella realized that this wasn't wind at all. Then from somewhere upstairs, the sound of a great pounding shook the house.

CHAPTER THIRTY-FIVE
SIMON

BOOM! BOOM! BOOM!

Simon wrapped his arm around Stella's. She didn't pull away.

Even Mr. Curtis looked startled.

BOOM!

"What *is* that?" Bev asked, her voice rising.

The walls rattled again. Harder this time. Was this what it had sounded like to Joshua when he'd been locked up in the attic that night? *Was* this Joshua? Still trapped here after all this time? Trying to get them to see him? Was this what *all* the strange occurrences had been about? The humming? The growling? The silhouettes, and the laughter?

The writing?

Certainly, Simon had noticed. Alex and Stella too. But maybe Joshua wanted more. Maybe he wanted the whole town to remember what had happened to him. Or would Ship Curtis be enough to appease him?

BOOM!

"It's coming from upstairs," said Alex, leading the group back into the foyer. They all looked up past the landing, at the darkness of the hallway beyond.

"Who's saying that?" Bev asked, rushing to the railing at the bottom step, tilting her head to listen.

Simon heard it too. Faint. As if it were coming from the third floor. From his attic bedroom. "Let me out! Please! Let me out of here!"

The front door slammed shut. Simon turned to find that Mr. Curtis was no longer with them. He'd heard Joshua's plea. And he'd run. Outside, the sound of a car engine hummed to life. Tires spit gravel as they peeled out.

BOOM!

Bev bolted up the stairs. Simon looked to the twins, who were both as surprised as he was. They all took off after her. At the top step, he noticed she'd hit the light switch. The bulb overhead blinked. The door that led up to the attic swung wide and hit the wall. Simon watched what looked like a blur of his stepmother disappearing through the doorway. He rushed to the door with Stella and Alex. They peered up the steep staircase. The sound was louder now. Simon took the steps quickly, though part of him — a large part — wanted to turn back and rush outside, like Mr. Curtis had. But when he reached the top and saw Bev staring at the wall beside his bed, he realized he was meant to be here.

With her.

With Stella and Alex.

Bev held her hands to the plaster. She faced them, her eyes wide and wet. "Is this another trick? Please tell me one of you isn't doing this."

"We swear," Simon said.

BOOM!

"But someone's in there," Bev said, gasping. "I can hear them. I can . . . *feel* them."

Someone, thought Simon. He stepped away from the group. Alex and Stella didn't notice as he rushed back to the stairs.

If they were going to get through that wall, they'd need a tool.

Luckily, Simon knew where to find one.

He stood before the staircase to the basement. He wished that he'd asked one of the twins to come with him. He still could. They were up in the attic.

BOOM!

No. He needed to do this now. He raced into the black, then ran through the passage, holding his hands over his head until they tangled with the cord hanging from the ceiling. He gave a hard pull, and the hallway awoke with light.

He skidded around the corner into the space where Dad kept some of his tools. Shadows pulled out from the walls. He exhaled a long, slow breath. His gaze slid over dim objects until he found the one he'd been looking for.

The shovel. Propped against the wall on the far side of the room. He padded across the dirt floor and grabbed it. The metal head was heavy. Before he could turn back, a creaking sound turned him to stone. From the corner of his eye, he saw the ancient door — the door that had started all this — swing open, revealing a kind of emptiness he didn't know existed.

The Cheaters' Room lay just beyond.

Simon looked into it, his heart slithering up his throat.

The darkness was peering back. He gripped the shovel and held it before him, like the paladin staff. If Joshua was making the commotion upstairs, then who was down here with him? Simon paused, as if something or someone might rush out from the doorway, grab him, pull him, screaming, into the room.

Then he ran. Around the corner. Into the light. Through the passage. Up the staircase to the foyer.

He slammed the basement door shut. The chair that the twins had used to trap him sat a few feet away. He pulled it over and shoved it against the knob.

BOOM!

Holding the edge of the banister, Simon flung himself toward the stairs so quickly, he nearly dropped the shovel. When he reached the landing, his father's voice called out from down by the front door. "Simon! What's going on?" But Simon couldn't stop to answer.

Upstairs, Bev, Stella, and Alex were attacking the plaster wall with their fists and feet.

BOOM! BOOM! BOOM!

"Watch out!" Simon yelled.

He rushed forward, swinging the shovel up over his head. Bev turned and scooted out of his way, pulling Stella and Alex with her. The blade broke through the plaster, cracks spidering outward. Simon tried to pull the shovel out, but it was stuck. He braced his feet against the bottom of the wall, then yanked harder. It gave a bit, but not much.

Stella joined on one side, Alex on the other. All three gripped the handle. They threw their weight backward and then tumbled down, the shovel clattering to the floor between them.

Bev approached the black hole they'd left behind. The booming had stopped. "Hello?" she said softly into the crevice. "We're . . . We're here now. You don't need to be scared anymore."

Simon helped his siblings to their feet.

Footfalls sounded on the stairs.

"What is happening up here?" Simon's father said, his face as worried as a wound.

CHAPTER THIRTY-SIX
ALEX

MOM TRIED TO tell Charlie everything. Or at least everything as she understood it.

Of course Charlie didn't believe it.

Well, it wasn't that he didn't believe it. He thought they'd all simply misunderstood the experience. "Some strange man comes in here with strange stories," he explained. "And then when you hear the building creaking in the wind, settling, as old places tend to do, you let your imaginations run wild."

"You weren't here, Charles," said Mom. *Charles.* Not Charlie. "You have no idea . . ."

Alex hated seeing them argue. So while they weren't paying attention, he picked up Simon's shovel and brought it over to the gouge they'd made. He swung it just like Simon had done. Plaster rained to the floor.

"Alex, please," Charlie groaned. He held out his hand. Alex handed over the shovel, then looked back to the wall. A wheezing came from the darkness inside. Alex knew he should put distance between himself and the hole, but they were all so close to finally learning the truth. Turning on all the lights. He reached out and pulled at the edges of the hole. Stella and Simon joined him. More and more plaster fell. Charlie gave up, gave in, and helped. Soon there was enough space for light to get through. Alex noticed what looked like an extension of the floorboards from Simon's bedroom on the other side of the wall.

"There's another room in there." Alex stood aside.

Charlie took his phone from his pocket, turned on the flashlight, then raised it toward the gash.

There was, in fact, another space beyond Simon's bedroom — a section of the old attic that had been left when someone, the previous owner maybe, had sealed it off.

After Charlie checked that the structure was sound, he waved the rest of them forward to pull away the old plaster. Soon they had created a doorway. Charlie entered first and gave the darkness a once-over. Alex watched the flashlight skirt over blackened surfaces, and if his eyes weren't playing tricks, he thought he saw writing on *these* walls as well. His mom brought a lamp from Simon's part of the attic and set it just inside the opening. Alex realized that this new scrawl had not been written in chalk like in the Cheaters' Room downstairs.

No, these letters had been scratched *into* the wood.

The same sentence. Over and over.

"LET ME OUT LET ME OUT LET ME OUT."

The space was not large. Maybe fifteen feet by twenty. Most of one side was made tight by the steep slope of the roof. Alex approached a spot where the wood looked newer, as if it had been repaired. Same with the floor underneath. He thought of what Mr. Curtis had told them.

About the storm.

And the fallen tree.

Here was the proof. The damage. The repair.

But not all of it could be repaired. Alex thought of the boy who hadn't survived.

Joshua.

When he felt someone brush against his arm, he nearly screamed. But it was only his sister. Simon had followed them, keeping close by, staring in awe at the black-painted wood, at the words scratched into them, at this place that had once been part of his bedroom.

The floor creaked as their parents moved farther, observing the junction where this part of the house met up with the north wing. Charlie looked almost shocked — his gaze wandering and his jaw slightly agape — as his theories of wild imaginations vaporized. Mom just looked relieved that the sounds had stopped.

Alex noticed an object caught between the floorboards not far from where he stood. He bent down to retrieve it but then noticed there were more. Slips of paper, folded, crumpled. He pulled one out and held it to the lamplight.

"You got this, Joshua."

The writing had been made with marker, slightly smeared by water and faded by time, but legible. He handed it to Stella. She stared at it, an amazed look on her face, as if this were a dream they were all sharing.

Simon ran over and knelt beside him. He removed another piece of paper. Stella sat and did the same. They read the messages aloud.

"We love you, Joshua."

"We believe you, Joshua."

"You'll be out in no time, buddy."

The more that Alex read, the more his eyes burned. He thought of the cards the family had received after his dad's funeral — the messages of hope and comfort — and how much they'd helped. How reading through them had made him feel less . . . *angry*.

The floor creaked behind him, and he realized that his parents were standing over them, reading along. Stella held up one of the messages to her mom. "Mr. Curtis was right."

Alex crawled to retrieve another stray paper a few feet farther away. He plucked at the corner that was sticking up from the floorboard. This one was stiffer and tricky to remove. When he'd managed to wiggle it halfway out, he realized that it was another Polaroid, like the one Gordon had found in the metal box in the barn. Gordon. Their supposed friend. Who'd had no problem setting them all up for the danger of this discovery. Alex wondered how he would respond when they told him what had happened tonight.

If they told him . . . He wasn't sure he wanted to speak to Gordon again anytime soon.

"What's that?" Simon asked.

"A picture," Alex said.

"Of who?" Stella wondered.

In the dim light, Alex hadn't been able to make it out. He brought it closer to the lamp. Two faces were visible. One of them, Alex recognized almost instantly. It was the girl from the first Polaroid. Peggy. She was smiling wide, her arm flung around the shoulder of someone who was most certainly a close friend. A boy. When Alex looked closer, he couldn't understand what he was seeing. The boy was smiling too. The strange thing was that Alex knew this smile as well, but not from any artifact they'd found around Wildwyck. No, this smile belonged to —

"Gordon?" Stella said, her voice a pinprick against a balloon.

She was right.

In the photograph, Peggy Wildwyck was hugging their friend Gordon Weinberger. Only there was writing on the white strip at the bottom, writing that revealed the boy must have had another name.

It read, *P + J ~ 1975.*

Peggy and Joshua.

And the year they'd died.

CHAPTER THIRTY-SEVEN
STELLA, ALEX & SIMON

LATER, IN THE den, Dad tried to explain it away.

"I *met* your friend Gordon," he said. "And yes, he looks very much like this boy in the photograph. But fathers have sons, remember. Uncles have nephews. Relatives across generations can look alike. We can't jump to conclusions based on a few strange pieces of paper we found in the attic."

"But you didn't hear what we heard, Charlie," Mom said. "You weren't here for that part."

The three kids couldn't believe she was actually taking their side.

"Can't we just call Gordon's house?" Alex suggested. "Ask him what he knows? Ask him . . . *who he is*?"

Charlie shook his head. "I'm not waking up some poor old woman for a wild-goose chase. We can look into this tomorrow."

Simon would not stay in the attic that night. Mom set up a mat and some blankets on the floor of Alex's room, and though it wasn't ideal, neither boy put up a fuss.

After midnight, there was a knock on the bedroom door. Since they'd both been staring at the ceiling, thoughts swirling like wind through the broken windows of Wildwyck's abandoned wings, both brothers sat up. Alex turned on the light. Simon's eyes were extra big, but when Alex nodded for him to answer the door, he scrambled over and whispered, "Who's there?"

"Let me in, doofuses," Stella said.

The three sat together on Alex's mattress, huddled around the metal box that Stella had brought with her. Inside, she'd placed all the messages they'd gathered up from between the attic floorboards, along with the new Polaroid marked *P + J*. By the soft light of Alex's bedside lamp, they compared the two images. Based on how Peggy was wearing her hair and the clothes she had on, they decided they must have been taken on the same day.

"How did this one get up to the attic?" Simon wondered, pinching the new picture between his thumb and forefinger, as if it were coated in poison.

Stella shrugged. "Maybe one of his friends took it from his room and slipped it under the attic door, just like the other letters."

"They look happy," said Alex. "Like they could have been brother and sister."

"Or really good friends," said Simon.

"Or both," said Stella. They sat in silence for a moment before she added, "Are we going to talk about . . ." The boys looked at her expectantly. She took the photo from Simon. "What if *Gordon* is our ghost? Gordon. Joshua. Whatever his name is?"

"*If ?*" Simon echoed. "There is no more *if.*"

"We need to figure out what he wants," Alex said. "I can't live in a haunted house."

"What if all he wanted was to be noticed?" Simon asked. "The sounds stopped when we found the Liars' Room. What if it's over?"

The twins thought about that. "I don't see how this answers the question of the writings on the basement walls," said Alex. "The lies we read there . . . Someone was trying to hurt us. Our family. Hurt us so bad that we'd . . . hate each other."

HATE . . . The word hung between them.

"There's something I need to tell you," Simon said quietly, breaking what felt like a spell. "It's the reason you two had a hard time making friends at Frost Meadow Middle School."

"You were spreading rumors?" Alex asked with a sneer.

"No," Simon said, trying to look serious. "I wouldn't — "

Stella interrupted him. "Yes, you would, and you know it."

"Maybe, but not anymore. Do you want to hear what I have to say or not?" The twins settled down, and Simon went on. "People were saying that you two were weird. They said you kept talking to yourselves in the hallways."

Stella and Alex glanced at each other. "Maybe we were. So what?"

"But, like, whole conversations. With someone who wasn't there."

Stella shivered. "Gordon?"

Alex swallowed hard. "Joshua."

"I don't know," Simon said. "But the kids who wanted

to hear my ghost stories were the same ones who told me you two were being creepy." He looked at the ceiling. "I . . . I didn't do much to correct them. I'm sorry."

The twins didn't know what to say. How could they just accept his apology after all that had happened?

After all he'd done?

After all they'd done to him?

The silence stretched out for longer than what felt comfortable. Finally, Stella spoke up. "I don't think I can sleep alone in my room tonight. Do you mind if I stay in here with you guys?"

Simon tossed her one of his blankets.

At school the next day, they each had a job to do.

Stella stopped by the main office first thing, and asked the secretary about a Frost Meadow student named Gordon Weinberger and where she might find his locker. Mrs. Vogel spent several minutes in the school's computer systems and, having no luck, searched the filing cabinets along the wall behind her desk. The woman returned, wearing a confused look. "Honey, are you sure you've got the right name? Seems there's no Gordon Weinberger at this school."

Alex approached his math teacher before class and showed him the photograph they'd found in the attic the night before. "I remember Peggy," said Mr. Levinthal, before squinting and looking closer. "But the boy . . . It *might* be Joshua Hendrix. What's this all about?" he asked. "Where'd you find this picture?" Alex mumbled an excuse as the bell rang, and Mr. Levinthal went back into math teacher mode.

During lunch, Simon snuck off to the library and asked his new friend, Ms. Mitchell, if he could use one of the computers. "Anytime," she answered, pressing her hand to her pocket as if to check for her phone. Simon did a search for a Gordon Weinberger in Frost Meadow, New York. The only item that popped up was the address for a Martha Weinberger, who lived in the village. Simon took down her phone number. Before the end of the day, he shared what he'd learned with Stella and Alex.

Stella stopped by the office again shortly after the last bell and asked if she could use the phone to call home. Mrs. Vogel agreed but not before giving her an exasperated look.

Mom picked up on the third ring. "Hello?" She sounded frantic, and Stella realized that the caller ID was showing that the number was from the school.

"Mom, it's me," Stella said quickly to quell her mother's nerves.

"What's wrong? You didn't miss the bus, did you?"

"Not yet. But Alex and Simon and I were wondering if you might pick us up today instead?"

Fifteen minutes later, just after the yellow buses had rumbled away from the lot, Mom's Subaru pulled up in front of the entrance. The kids got in. She looked at them apprehensively. "You sure you want to do this?"

Stella nodded. "We don't have a choice."

CHAPTER THIRTY-EIGHT
STELLA, ALEX & SIMON

THE WEINBERGER HOUSE was a five-minute drive from the school.

When Mom parked at the curb across the street, none of them moved to get out. "Should we call first?" Stella asked. "Make sure she's home?"

"And if she's not?" Alex said. "Do we leave a note?"

"Let's ring the doorbell and see," Simon said.

Mom glanced at the three, as if seeing them in a new light. After a moment, she opened the driver's door. "Well, we're not getting anything done sitting here," she said.

Alex, Stella, and Simon followed her across the street to the white cottage. The front was overfilled with rose-bushes, the last of the red blossoms clinging onto the end of the swiftly changing season. The wide porch was loaded with dusty wicker furniture and a few crumpled cardboard boxes. As the group climbed the steps, a tabby cat glanced up from one of the chairs.

Stella was hugging the metal box to her chest, so Alex had to press the dirty button beside the doorknob. A harsh bell sounded from somewhere inside. They waited quietly for a few moments, glancing at one another with worried looks, before Simon reached out and tried again. This time there was a shout. "Hold yer horses!"

An elderly woman opened the heavy wood door and stared at them through the closed screen. Her silver hair was short, styled in neat curls close to her scalp. Her eyes were dark and her skin was pink. She wore a violet pullover hoodie and loose jeans. She seemed surprised — and slightly suspicious — to have so many visitors. "What's this about?" she asked, looking to Mom at the edge of the porch.

The three kids stared at the old woman, afraid and excited for the answers she might have.

Alex spoke up, "Are you Mrs. Weinberger?"

"I am," the woman answered, an edge in her voice.

"Do you know someone named Gordon?"

She hesitated before saying, "I do."

This could have meant so many things.

Stella sensed that she was about to ask them all to leave. Feeling brave, she pronounced, "Mrs. Weinberger, we have some questions about him. This might sound weird, but we'd really appreciate it if you gave us the time. Can we . . . come in?"

Mrs. Weinberger shook her head. "I'm sorry, but my house is an absolute wreck. No one visits." Then she opened the screen door. "But if you don't mind pushing Tessie off her favorite spot, I suppose we could gather out here. But not for too long. One of my shows is starting soon."

Tessie went without a fuss.

They introduced themselves. Mrs. Weinberger threw a questioning look to Mom, and Mom, surprisingly, just smiled and let the kids do their thing.

None of them thought it was a good idea to start off with

the scary stuff right away. "Gordon is your grandson?" Stella asked.

Mrs. Weinberger *tsked*. "Gordon is my *son*."

"Oh. We thought . . . Is he . . . *home*?"

"Gordon lives in Chicago. He and his husband are lawyers. Last time I saw them was over Fourth of July weekend. Why do you want to know?" She glanced again at Mom. They were losing her.

"Show her the Polaroid," Simon whispered.

Stella opened the metal box. She handed the photograph to the old woman. Mrs. Weinberger tilted her head to look at it slanted through her glasses. She held the Polaroid steady, examining the two kids in the picture. She looked up. "What is this?"

"Is the boy in the photograph your son?" Alex asked.

"I've already told you. My son is grown."

"Does the boy in the photograph *look* like your son?" Simon tried.

A troubled look came upon her. "Where did you get this?"

"We found it in our house," Stella answered. "At Wildwyck."

Mrs. Weinberger's lips parted with a soft click. "The old school."

Mom nodded. "My husband and I are fixing it up."

"Quite a task." Did she mean the workload? Or was she talking about something else? "My Gordon went there, you know. Long time ago." *Now* they were getting somewhere. Mrs. Weinberger waggled the Polaroid at them. "Gordon was friends with the boy in this picture."

"So then, you *do* recognize him?" Alex asked.

"Oh yes." She nodded slowly. "How could I forget? After what happened . . ." Another pause, and then, "This boy . . . Joshua, was his name. Joshua Hendrix. And Peggy. Poor girl. Except for her, my Gordon was that boy's best friend. Maybe his *only* other friend. Gordon had a Polaroid camera back then. I wouldn't be surprised if he was the one who took this photo."

Stella nearly dropped the metal box from her lap. Simon held his hands to his mouth. Alex felt the need to turn and run, but then composed himself and leaned forward instead. Mom folded her arms uncomfortably, shifting her weight in the wicker chair.

"Why would you have thought that Joshua was my Gordon?" the old woman asked.

Mom spoke up. "My kids have come across a few interesting items around the house over the past few weeks. Things tend to get uncovered when you're knocking down walls. We've learned some names of old students and faculty — even Peggy Wildwyck and her family. We've been . . . trying to piece it together."

"There's an old graveyard out behind the barn," Simon added, as creepy as ever.

"I know where it is," Mrs. Weinberger said, not missing a beat. "I attended Peggy's service there. With Gordon, actually."

The group was quiet for a moment.

"We heard . . . Joshua Hendrix died in an accident at the school," said Stella.

"Awful." Mrs. Weinberger nodded. "The Wildwycks cut

down most of the trees surrounding the school after that. They had very little to say about the . . . the rest of it. Word spread around the village . . . Well, no need to sugarcoat at this point. They were abusive. It was unacceptable. I pulled Gordon from their school. It stayed open for only a few more years. Once the state got word, they yanked funding so fast, the Wildwycks could barely stand, never mind run that place."

Another moment of silence.

Alex spoke up. "Mrs. Weinberger, do you know . . . Where did Joshua Hendrix end up?"

The old woman gave a slight nod. "He was a ward of the state. An orphan. The least the Wildwycks could do was offer him a spot in which he could rest."

Simon squeaked, "You mean — "

"He's out in the woods too."

"In the family plot?" Stella asked.

"Not quite. If I recall, his grave was a bit farther. The Wildwycks didn't tell many people. I only heard because I played organ for the church. Even so, I'm not sure if the family had a ceremony for him. The poor boy."

A screeching echoed through the porch: "LET ME OUT LET ME OUT LET ME OUT." Then two sparrows flew up from the rosebushes, squawking at each other before flittering away to a nearby tree. Startled, Stella fought to catch her breath. "Would you know where we could find him? His grave?" She looked to the metal box. "We have some of his things. We think . . ." She paused, trying to figure out how to word what she wanted to say, but then realized she didn't care how it sounded. "We think he might want them back."

CHAPTER THIRTY-NINE
STELLA, ALEX & SIMON

IT TOOK SOME time, but they eventually found the stone about twenty feet past the clearing, under the shadowed canopy of the tallest trees. A small lump of a rock, mostly smooth, almost flat, the initials and date painted in red, now chipped. *J. H. '75*

Mom and Dad couldn't deny it any longer. Joshua Hendrix had lived at Wildwyck. He'd died there too. After what each of them had seen, they also came to understand that he'd never left.

By the end of the week, they'd made the arrangements.

On Saturday morning, mist was lying low in the meadows, but the sky was a blue September gift. The trees surrounding Wildwyck were still mostly green, but the colder nights had been daring warmer colors to wake.

Stella wore a dark dress with tiny red dots, and she pulled her hair back into a neat ponytail.

Alex put on his nicest pants and one of his father's old ties.

Simon dressed in black pajamas and dress shoes. "They're the only black clothes I own at the moment," he explained. Stella and Alex knew enough to not argue. He wasn't doing it to annoy them. Or to annoy anyone. He was just being himself. And how could they be mad about that? Alex did, however, mark down the words *Black Pajamas* in the Notes app, certain they would make a good title for something.

Shortly after eleven, several cars pulled into the driveway. Mom and Dad, who'd also managed to clean up for the occasion, greeted the guests with cups of coffee. Stella, Alex, and Simon carried the items they'd prepared. Stella held the metal box. Alex brought folded-paper programs. And Simon clenched copies of the P + J Polaroid so tightly, he'd creased their corners.

"Hi, Mr. Levinthal," Alex said to his teacher.

Stella greeted the real Gordon's mother. "Thanks for coming, Mrs. Weinberger."

"Nice of you to return, Mr. Curtis." Simon saluted the bookshop owner. "Sorry about last time."

Mr. Levinthal, Mrs. Weinberger, and Mr. Curtis each accepted a program and a picture. Then, with coffee in hand, they made their way up the path beside the stone wall, past the barn, and into the woods.

In the clearing, the leaves rustled overhead so harshly, it sounded like the trees were gossiping. The group followed the kids out of the sunlight and into the shadows until they reached the spot where Joshua's stone waited. The three had worked hard all week cleaning away layers of dead leaves, pulling out weeds and brush so that the site resembled the ones in the family plot. Stella didn't think grass would ever grow here — it was too shaded. But they could keep Joshua's grave looking nice for as long as Wildwyck was home.

Alex began. "We've gathered today to remember someone

who lived here once, a long time ago. Someone who deserves
to be remembered. Joshua Hendrix. This spot is where he's
buried."

All three had discussed it. This is what they believed
the haunting had been about. And this was what they hoped
would put it to an end. Alex nodded to Stella.

She opened the box and passed around the pieces of brittle paper they'd discovered almost a week prior. "If you all
wouldn't mind reading your message aloud . . ." She blushed.
She wasn't sure what she was doing. The only memorial she'd
ever been to had been her father's. "I'll start." She read the
writing. *"Joshua, we're here for you."* She glanced at Simon.

"The darkness in that room won't last forever," Simon read,
looking around at the group. His stomach felt shaky, but when
Mom and Dad smiled at him, he managed to smile back.

Now it was Alex's turn. *"Wherever Peggy is, she's thinking
of you."* He looked to the photocopy of the Polaroid, saw the
two faces peering back at him, as if across time.

As if they could see him too.

Mom and Dad read their messages, followed quickly by
the others. Stella, Alex, and Simon didn't know what else to
say, so they decided to leave it at that. Alex gathered up the
scraps and organized them in a short stack.

They'd brought out a small spade the day before. Stella
lifted her skirt slightly and then knelt in the dirt. The boys
followed. Placing the metal box beside herself, she and her
brothers dug a hole deep enough and wide enough for it to fit
inside. She took the scraps from Alex and set them in the box,

along with the P + J photograph. Together, the three filled in the hole and, using their hands, covered the box. They patted it flat and smoothed it out. Looking at the patch of ground, you would never have known something was buried there.

CHAPTER FORTY

November 25

It feels weird finally being here after everything they say happened. But I have this week off from school, so Mom thought it would be a good idea to put me on a plane and send me to New York.

I can see why Simon says Wildwyck was haunted. The building itself is creepier than creepy.

But then, according to everyone, the ghost seems to have left. Or if not left, he's decided to leave them alone. A good thing, since so much of what happened here seemed to be based around me. And my journal.

How did the ghost even know I keep a journal, I wonder?

Maybe Simon told him. Blabbermouth.

The strangest part about coming to Frost Meadow isn't even the ghost stories. The strangest part is walking into a family that I don't recognize. Not that it's a bad thing to have your stepsiblings getting along with your troublesome little brother.

At first, I thought it was a joke. A put-on. The way they were all behaving. But nope. The twins actually seem to <u>like</u> Simon now. And vice versa. All it took to bring them together was their house being haunted.

And they say ghosts are a bad thing . . .

But somehow, it makes me feel like I've stumbled into a

rehearsal for a play where everyone knows their lines but me. Like, if I don't pay close enough attention, they'll all just move on to the next scene, and I'll be lost in the dark.

The first thing we did when I arrived on Monday afternoon was help Stella finish up this weird mural in her bedroom. I told her I have no clue how to even hold a brush, but she didn't care. She'd already sketched the image onto the wall next to her bed. A sort of paint-by-number unicorn with ice-cream clouds. And rainbows. Lots and lots of rainbows. Thank goodness for the rainbows. Those are easy enough to fudge. By the end of the afternoon, Stella was so giddy about it, the rest of us couldn't help but laugh along at how big she was smiling.

Then yesterday, they showed me all the spooky spots. Like the haunted tour you can sign up for at that theater in Columbus. Simon and Stella and Alex were the guides. They wanted me to see every creepy place where every creepy thing went down.

I took pictures, so it would seem like I was just as excited about it as they were. To be honest, I thought it was pretty weird. Especially when they took me out behind the barn and into the woods. Reading the names carved into the gravestones made it all seem suddenly very real. At home, in Ohio, when Simon would tell me his stories over video chat, I could keep them at a distance. But here. Seeing it all with my own eyes. You know that these names belonged to actual people. It no longer felt like just a story you might tell your friends for fun. These people were dead. Their bones buried just below where we were standing.

It couldn't be any more _real_ than that.

Scary stuff has always been one of the ways that me and Simon *have been similar, ever since we were little. Movies. Books. Video games. Now here at Wildwyck, I'm not sure how I feel about it anymore. Especially not at night, in the attic, sleeping on the cot in the corner, listening to Simon snore.*

I don't know how he does it. All that separates him now from the place they called the Liars' Room is a bit of cardboard, nailed up over the smashed plaster. Dad offered to show me what's on the other side, but I said no.

I know it's weird, but I decided to come down to the basement, to spend some time in the room where all the trouble started. The place where they found the chalk writing on the walls. Words that were meant to belong to me. I crept down the stairs when no one was looking. Turned on the hall light, then around the corner, I flicked on the flashlight on my phone. The old wooden door stood open. That writing is gone now, but you can still sense it.

I keep thinking how Simon said there were three bad rooms in the old school. If the Liars' Room is in the attic, and the Cheaters' Room is in the basement, I wonder where the Temper Room is. Dad didn't mention finding it yet. I wonder if good ol' Joshua Hendrix spent any time there as well. They better figure it out before they start putting up drywall. I definitely wouldn't want to be the one whose bedroom turned out to be a place that used to be covered in foam mats so that angry preteen boys wouldn't hurt themselves by punching and kicking and spitting and raging at nothing.

At nothing.

I can't help wondering, if a ghost did put those words there, in the Cheaters' Room, what were they trying to achieve? I mean, the

*family seems happy with the idea of making peace. They found the
room where Joshua died. And they put his soul to rest, tucked softly
into the ground. There's something that bothers me though.*

*It's like they're forgetting the part where Joshua — if he's the
one who did all this — was not some sad little thing who was
looking for remembrance. No.*

*The spirit made noise. The spirit growled. Pounded the walls.
Moved furniture. Laughed when it knew they were scared.*

*Maybe Joshua felt hurt by what had happened to him during
his life. Maybe, in death, he was lashing out. Maybe he was jeal-
ous that a family had moved in here, a family like he'd never had.
Maybe he wanted to hurt them so badly that they wouldn't have
been a family any longer.*

*And how easily they forgave him. It's like they think that once
Dad erased the words from the walls of this room, he erased the
pain and the fear that those words had caused, as well as the pain
and fear that had caused them.*

*And if Joshua <u>wasn't</u> as innocent as they all wanted to believe,
maybe erasing his words only made him angrier.*

*Maybe Joshua's as angry as I am now. Angry that I got left
behind in Ohio. Angry that Simon likes his stepsiblings better
than he likes me. Angry that the family is moving on. That I'm no
longer part of the conversation. That I feel invisible. Forgotten.
Unseen. Maybe Joshua and I have more in common than any of
the rest of them could imagine.*

*I wonder what they'll think when one of them comes back
down here to the Cheaters' Room and reads this new journal entry.*

*Charlie painted over the other writings, but he left the chalk
behind. I found a piece lying on the floor in the dirt. All I had to*

do was brush it off and start again. I wonder what they'll think when they get to this very part, the words that I'm laying out right now. Will they wonder if <u>Zachary</u> would try and throw them off this time? Will they wonder if their son is capable of trying to do to them the same thing they believed a ghost had done? To frighten them? To hurt them? To try and break them apart?

Or maybe they'll wonder if Joshua Hendrix is still the author . . .

Will reading these words make the family wonder if the show they put on out in the woods didn't actually work? Reciting those messages at the grave. Burying the Polaroid. Covering the old metal box with cold earth.

I'll bet that when they get to this part, they'll feel the same chill I used to feel in my bones just after the Wildwycks planted me, a measured six feet down.

Maybe, after they go back upstairs, they'll start to worry that the noises will begin again. The humming. The pounding. The crying. The growling. Maybe they'll wonder what they did wrong. And what they can do to try to fix it again.

But what if there is no way to fix this? Because what if whoever is writing these words isn't Joshua? What if more graves are hidden out in the woods beyond his? What if more students disappeared at Wildwyck over the years?

Kids who spent time in other dark rooms.

Behind other locked doors.

Maybe these words belong to one of them.

It's not beyond the realm of possibility. Not anymore. You must understand that now. After everything you've been through. After everything you've seen. After reading what I've written on these walls.

This is a funny question, I think. The question of who I am. Funny, because even if someone tells you the truth, at this point, you might not believe them. Even after everything, there will be doubt.

You opened the door. Did you truly believe it could be closed again? Even if you tried, you'd always know what is inside. And that's the point. Isn't it? Words and deeds often remain, even if only in memory. Like bloodstains on ancient stone, lies cannot be washed away.

It's something to keep in mind while you sit around that big table, eating your dinner, looking into the faces of your company, your family, wondering who among them would have dared.

Or maybe it was, and always has been, little old me,

Your friend.

ACKNOWLEDGMENTS

I NEED TO wish many thanks to everyone who helped me put this book together. Matthew Sawicki listened to the entire plot one night on a bike ride around town and encouraged me through some doubts. Talia Seidenfeld's sharp editorial vision was an absolute blessing. Thanks to Erin Black and Nick Eliopulos for early encouragement. The team at Scholastic has been a dream, as always—special thanks to Janell Harris, Julia Eisler, Rachel Feld, Christopher Stengel, and everyone else who had their grubby little hands in *Liars' Room*. Shout out to Barry Goldblatt. I'm incredibly pleased that Glynn Washington from the *Snap Judgment* and *Spooked* podcasts allowed me to use his quote for the epigraph; thank you to Marisa Dodge, who pointed me toward the season and episode number. And a big thank you to Michael Bourret.

I lost a dear friend in the middle of creating this book. I would not be the person I am today if not for Charles Beyer. Some aspect of Charlie has accidentally made it into every single story I've ever written. I will miss you, CGB, always, always. Thank you for everything.